The Millionaire's Wish

ABIGAIL STROM

MILLS & BOON

First published in Great Britain 2011
by Mills & Boon, an imprint of Harlequin (UK) Limited,
Large Print edition 2011
Eton House, 18-24 Paradise Road,
Richmond, Surrey TW9 1SR

© Abigail Strom 2011

ISBN: 978 0 263 22272 2

Harlequin (UK) policy is to use papers that are natural,
renewable and recyclable products and made from
wood grown in sustainable forests. The logging
and manufacturing process conform to the legal
environmental regulations of the country of origin.

Printed and bound in Great Britain
by CPI Antony Rowe, Chippenham, Wiltshire

ABIGAIL STROM

started writing stories at the age of seven and has never been able to stop. She's thrilled to be published by Mills & Boon. She works full-time as a human resources professional and lives in New England with her family, who are incredibly supportive of the hours she spends hunched over her computer. She loves hearing from readers and can be reached at abigail@abigailstrom.com.

To my husband

Authors are often encouraged to
write what they know.
Thanks to you,
when I write about true love…I am

Chapter One

"How hard would it be to rob a bank?"

Allison Landry frowned at the financial statements covering her desk. One of her volunteers, who also was one of her best friends, had just come into the office with a letter in her hand.

"That bad, huh?" Rachel asked sympathetically.

"Or maybe we could pull off a jewel heist."

"We could wear black leather catsuits," Rachel suggested. "And hire a professional thief to help us. You know, like the guys in *Ocean's Eleven*. Preferably a George Clooney look-alike. I'd also be willing to consider Brad Pitt."

Allison's mouth tipped up in a smile. "I'd go with Cary Grant in *To Catch a Thief*, but then I'm old-fashioned."

Rachel laughed. "I'm liking this idea more and more." She paused. "Okay, fill me in for real. What's going on?"

Allison sighed, closing her eyes briefly as she ran both hands through her short brown hair. "It's been a bad day. Kevin Buckley is in the hospital again—I heard from his parents this morning. And our financial outlook for the coming year is pretty grim. Donations have been down ever since the recession started, so we're going to have to cut back on some of our existing services. And we'll have to put the plans for Megan's House on hold again—indefinitely, this time. It'll be a struggle to keep some of our programs going at all, and it's not the time to start something new."

She felt the disappointment all over again as she spoke the reality out loud. For years she'd cherished the dream of building a retreat center for families dealing with childhood cancer. She'd hoped the dream was close to being realized, but the bleak financial picture in front of her said otherwise.

"It'll happen someday," she said now, half to Rachel and half to herself. She couldn't let her determination be quenched. After all, this wasn't the first time she'd had to face harsh realities. When you lost a sister to cancer—Megan had been just fourteen when she died—you also lost any illusion that life was fair.

"I'm sorry," Rachel said, and Allison knew she really meant it. Still, her expression was more unhappy than the occasion warranted.

"Does the look on your face have something to do with that letter in your hand?"

Rachel nodded. "I hate to give you more bad news. It's about Julie's wish."

Allison frowned. "But that's the easiest one we've had in ages. She just wants to meet that software CEO—the man who designed that video game she likes so much. Rick Hunter, right? He lives right here in Des Moines. What's the problem?"

Rachel shrugged her shoulders helplessly. "He turned us down."

Allison just stared at her. "That's ridiculous. He doesn't even have to get on a plane. His company owns that big office building on Grand. He could walk to the hospital, for goodness' sake."

"He could, but he won't. He sent us a donation instead."

A donation. Of course.

Not that the money wasn't welcome. As her financial statements clearly showed, they needed every donation they could get.

But she was willing to bet this wasn't the first time Rick Hunter, president and CEO of Hunter Systems, had pulled out his checkbook instead of volunteering his time.

And now he was trying to buy his way out of visiting a cancer patient.

"Let me see that," Allison said, and Rachel handed it to her.

"Must regretfully decline your request... busy professional...demands on my time..."

She crumpled the letter into a ball and threw it toward the wastebasket. She missed by two feet. "Busy professional, he says. Can you *believe* that? We got the quarterback of the Green Bay Packers to visit one of our kids last year, and that was during football season!"

It had been a lousy day, and even though only part of her current frustration was really directed at Rick Hunter, he was her most convenient target at the moment.

Extremely convenient, in fact. As in a five minute drive from her office.

She shoved her chair back and rose to her feet.

"You look really pissed off," Rachel said warily. "You're not going to do anything crazy, are you?"

"That depends on your definition of crazy. I'm just going to have a little chat with—"

Rachel's eyes widened. "You're going to yell at him. You're going to yell at Rick Hunter. Allison, you can't do that!"

"I can't, huh? Give me one good reason," Allison said, turning off her computer and grabbing her purse.

Rachel was at her own desk now, rifling through file folders and stacks of papers. "He's rich, for one thing. Like potential platinum donor rich. He designed the most popular video game in the world. He's important."

"Julie's important, too."

"Of course she is. I just think—got it!" she announced suddenly, holding up an issue of *People* magazine.

"What's so exciting about that?"

Rachel opened the magazine to a two-page profile—picture on the left and a short biography on the right.

"America's Most Eligible Bachelors," she said, as if that explained everything.

"I take it Rick Hunter made the list."

"I'll say. Allison, just look at him. You'll have to agree there are better things to do with this man than yell at him."

Allison rolled her eyes, but when Rachel brought the picture over she glanced at it to satisfy her.

Rick Hunter was on an unmade bed, leaning back on his elbows with a slight smile on his face, as if he found the person holding the camera mildly amusing. He was wearing a tuxedo, jacket off and tie loosened. That, along with the stubble on his jaw and the artfully tousled black hair, gave him an air of casual decadence, as if he'd recently enjoyed a very good time in that bed.

His eyes weren't as casual as the rest of him. They were green, and the expression in them was reserved, even remote, but with a kind of intensity in their depths that probably had most women ready to fall at his feet.

In spite of herself, she found herself looking into those eyes a shade longer than she meant to. When she realized it, she took the magazine from Rachel's outstretched hand and tossed it back onto her desk.

"I admit he's decorative," she said. "So what? I hope you're not saying I should be nice to Rick Hunter because you think he's cute."

"Puppies are cute. Kittens are cute. This man is *gorgeous.* I'm talking drop-dead, stop-the-presses, melt-your-knees gorgeous."

"You forgot to mention spoiled, selfish, arrogant—"

"I don't think he's like that," Rachel objected. "Did you look at the article? He—"

"I'm not interested," Allison said firmly. "He turned down a kid with cancer. There's no possible excuse for that, and I'm going to tell him so."

Rachel grabbed her hand as she headed for the door. "You have to go home and change first."

Allison glanced down at herself. She was wearing a typical outfit for a day when she had no meetings with hospital directors or wealthy philanthropists—jeans and a blue flannel shirt. Her feet were clad in an old pair of tennis shoes.

"I'm not going all the way back to my apartment to change clothes. Why, do you think his office has a dress code?"

"Very funny." Rachel grabbed her purse and

started looking through it. "At least let me put some makeup on you. Lipstick, mascara, something. Your face is all naked!"

"Sorry," Allison said firmly. "This is going to be a come-as-you-are meeting."

Rachel put her purse back on her desk. "There isn't a woman alive who wouldn't primp before going to see Rick Hunter. You're not normal, Allison."

"I've heard that before."

"And yet, I still love you." Rachel sighed. "Have fun storming the castle."

Rick Hunter held the phone away from his ear as he typed one-handed, listening to his grandmother with half his attention while he focused on a complicated spreadsheet.

"—and it's not that I'm *prudish*—I was a bit of a rebel in my time, I'll have you know. Your grandfather could tell you stories. Well, he could if he were alive. But I do not appreciate half the people I know calling me to discuss this appalling magazine article, which refers to you as 'The Playboy of the Midwest,' I might add."

Rick winced. He'd only done that damn photo shoot because of his company's upcoming annual charity event, a ball at the Grand Hotel to be followed by a bachelor auction. He wasn't participating—he never did, despite his undeniable bachelor status—but the magazine, along with his marketing director, had convinced him it would be great publicity for the event if the company president was in the article.

"I didn't write the copy, Gran. And I told you before—"

She spoke right over him. "I wouldn't be so upset if it didn't confirm what I always suspected. You have no intention of ever settling down, have you?"

He was correcting a complicated cell formula and missed the question. "What?"

"I said, you have no intention of ever settling down. The women you involve yourself with! The fluffy, brainless ones are bad enough, but the ruthless corporate types are even worse. I actually look forward to the straightforward gold diggers you toss into the mix occasionally. Not one of the girls you've dated in the last five years has been someone I'd be proud to call my granddaughter. Not that I've had cause to worry, since you've never shown the slightest interest in committing to any of them."

Rick sighed. "Okay, Gran, so you don't like the women I date. But neither of us has to put up with them on a long-term basis, so what's your problem?"

"My problem is that my only grandson is still a bachelor! You don't think I dream of the day you'll settle down here with your wife and children?"

Here meant the Hunter estate, of course. The beautiful old mansion his great-great-grandfather had built in 1890. Not the house Rick had grown up in, but the only place he'd ever thought of as home. The only place he'd ever truly been happy.

"The fact is," she went on, "I've been thinking things over. And I'm considering giving Hunter Hall to your second cousin."

Rick's hand froze over the keyboard. "What?"

"You heard me. Jeremiah and his wife are planning to have children, and they'd like to raise their family here. They've said so."

Rick's jaw tightened. "If Jeremiah's shown any interest, it's because of what the house might be worth on the open market. He and his wife don't give a damn about the place. They'll sell it, Gran."

She sniffed. "That's not what they've told me. And even if they thought that at one time, things change once you decide to have a family."

She paused, and Rick thought about what it would mean to lose Hunter Hall. Maybe he'd never told Gran, but he loved it more than any place on earth.

"This house cries out for children. If I thought there was a chance you might change your ways…"

His grandmother had been hoping to marry him off for years. He, on the other hand, had never been interested in marriage. His own parents hadn't exactly been a shining example of the institution, and he had no intention of repeating their mistakes. Better to stay clear of all that and focus on things you could actually control. Like work.

Even if work hadn't been very satisfying lately.

Rick leaned back in his chair, staring at his computer screen. If work was getting stale it was his own fault, and was therefore something he could fix. He owned the damn company, after all.

A marriage, on the other hand, wasn't something one person could control. Two hearts, two minds, two egos—and way too much risk. Date for fun, that was his motto—and when the fun started to fade, end things quick and clean, before either party had too much invested. And yes, that meant that he tended to date women he wasn't likely to fall for.

"I just want to see you happy, Richard."

"I am happy." Or content, anyway. He'd never expected happiness. His life was going according to plan, and he had no desire to make any changes. The only thing he wanted that he didn't already have was Hunter Hall.

"Won't you at least think about what I've

said? It wouldn't kill you to date a woman of character for once."

Rick smiled at the old-fashioned phrase. "And what would a 'woman of character' want with me?" He'd meant it as a joke, but his voice sounded a little bitter in his own ears.

His grandmother sighed. "If you don't know the answer already, it won't do any good to tell you. I'm sorry about Hunter Hall, dear, but I need to believe that this house will echo with the voices of children someday."

Rick looked at the opposite wall, where the original advertisement for "Magician's Labyrinth" hung in a mahogany frame. He'd modeled the magician's house after Hunter Hall, and the image had been part of the game's cover art ever since.

"It's your house, Gran. You can do whatever you want with it."

"I just wish you'd consider—"

"Yeah. I have to get back to work, okay? I'll talk to you soon."

But he didn't get back to work. He leaned back in his chair, frowning at his spreadsheet without really seeing it.

Maybe this was for the best. Wanting something you couldn't achieve through your own efforts was a weakness, and Rick had never tolerated weakness.

His paperweight was a replica of the magician's house carved out of stone, a gift from his gaming programmers a few years ago. He picked it up now, feeling the smooth, compact weight of it in his palm.

The thought of losing Hunter Hall made something clench inside him, as if his internal organs were being put through a wringer. His grip tightened. The peaks of the roof cut into his skin, and he knew this one childhood dream still had a hold on him.

His private line lit up. He set the paperweight

back down on his desk and put his assistant on speaker. "What is it, Carol?"

"I'm sending a woman in to see you." She sounded irritated, but then she always did. After six years, he still wasn't sure if the irritation was for the world in general or him in particular.

He frowned. "You know I'm preparing for the product review tomorrow. Who is it you want to send in?"

"Someone from that foundation. The one that runs the Wish Upon a Star program."

He felt a twinge of guilt. That girl—Jenny or Julie or something. She was undergoing cancer treatment, and she wanted to meet him. Her request had come in a letter from a nonprofit agency, explaining who they were and what they did, and asking if they could arrange a hospital visit on the girl's behalf.

"I told you to decline their request and send them a check."

"Which I did, *mon capitaine.* But someone has come in person to speak with you about the matter. A Ms. Allison Landry."

"Ms. Landry is out of luck. Send her on her way."

"No."

His eyebrows drew together. "What do you mean, no?"

"Look, boss. There may be assistants out there who could turn away a righteous woman trying to help a girl with cancer, but I am not one of them. I'm sending Ms. Landry in."

Rick felt another twinge of guilt, but he refused to give in to it. He had no desire to visit a cancer ward and his reasons were no one's business. And he'd had it up to here with righteous women today, between his grandmother and Carol and now this latest interruption.

He pictured her as a woman with iron gray hair and an iron gray demeanor, and the thought of her invading his inner sanctum and scowling at him in disapproval was too damn irritating to deal with.

"I'm in a bad mood. If she comes in here I'll just snarl at her."

Carol snorted. "This one can take it. She'll snarl right back."

Definitely iron gray.

Rick sighed. "Fine. Go ahead and send her in."

He barely had time to rise to his feet before his door opened and Allison Landry stepped into his office.

Never in his life had a preconceived image been so off the mark. The woman coming toward him was hardly more than a girl—a girl whose short, silky haircut made her look like an angry pixie.

She had a pixie's body, too—at least what he could see of it. Her slender, understated curves weren't exactly showcased by her jeans and flannel shirt.

This was not a woman who used her appearance to get what she wanted. She didn't even wear makeup, he noted as she came to a halt in front of his desk, her eyes blazing and her cheeks flushed.

Not that she needed it. She had perfect skin—so clear and smooth he found himself wondering if it could possibly feel as soft as it looked.

Her eyes didn't need any help, either. They were the color of—what was the name of that stone? Lapis lazuli? And fringed by eyelashes so thick they were like tiny black fans.

Her mouth…her mouth was pretty good too. Wide and full and sweet, even with the corners turned down as she registered her obvious dislike of everything about him.

She looked mad as hell. And the fact that he was a rich and powerful CEO was not going to stop her from telling him about it.

* * *

Allison rode her wave of anger right into the executive office. And there was Rick Hunter, rising to his feet to meet her, every hair in place and with no hint of stubble along his jaw.

He was all business, exuding the same power and sophistication as the mahogany and leather furniture that had probably set him back what Allison paid in office rent for a year. She couldn't even imagine what the suit cost. She'd always thought that computer executives had a more casual look, but Rick Hunter obviously preferred formality.

Probably because it kept people at a distance.

"Mr. Hunter," she began coldly. "I came here to—"

He came around to the front of his desk, and she backed up a pace or two before she could stop herself. He was tall, about eight inches taller than her five foot six, and the difference made her feel at a disadvantage. "You're from the Star Foundation?" he asked.

"I'm the director. And I—"

"The director?" He leaned back against his desk. "You look about eighteen."

"I'm twenty-seven," she said in a voice like ice. "Want to see my driver's license?"

A corner of his mouth twitched. "That's all right. I believe you." He studied her for a moment, his green eyes appraising. "You're here because I turned down that girl's request. I suppose you think I owe you an apology."

Her spine stiffened. "You don't owe me a damn thing, and I'm not interested in an apology. I'm only interested in knowing when you're going to visit Julie. I know you're a busy professional with demands on your time—" she didn't even try to curb the sarcasm in her voice "—and that the request of a stranger doesn't loom large on your to-do list. Especially when it would involve spending an entire hour devoted to something other than business or your own pleasure—"

He raised his hands, palms out. "Slow down, Ms. Landry. I don't—"

"And I'm sure you're not used to sacrificing even that much time to make someone else happy. But if you had any idea what these kids go through on a daily basis—the hell their families live through—"

"I do," he said roughly, and when she stopped in surprise, staring at him, he looked away. That was actually a relief, as she found herself strangely distracted by those green eyes, which the photographer, good as he or she had been, hadn't done justice to.

"I mean," he said more quietly, "I can imagine. And despite what you obviously think of me, I didn't turn down your request because I'm a selfish, uncaring bastard. My reasons—" he stopped. "My reasons are none of your business. But I'd be more than happy to make a sizable donation to your foundation, and if you choose to use some of those funds to get something for Jenny—"

"Her name is Julie." She was so mad her skin felt hot. "It might interest you to know that most of our kids don't wish for *things*. Most of their wishes have to do with people—wanting to meet a favorite writer or athlete or musician. Wanting to meet someone they admire."

That made him frown. "Why would Julie admire *me?*"

"Didn't you read her letter? You designed her favorite game, and she loves it. It's helped her through a terrible time in her life. Something about the game connected with her, and because of that, she feels connected to you. She'd like to meet you. Why is that so hard to understand? And why on earth can't you take an hour or two out of your day to—"

"No," he said abruptly. "I'm sorry to disappoint you—and her—but that's not going to be possible. Now, why don't we discuss that donation I mentioned? I'm sure an agency like yours needs every—"

"I'm not interested in your money."

The words came out impulsively. She knew she'd regret them tomorrow. Even now a voice was telling her not to be stupid, not to be proud, and to take Rick Hunter's guilt money. People who ran nonprofits couldn't afford to be choosy, and plenty of donations were made for publicity, or for the tax deduction, or for any number of reasons that had nothing to do with the foundation's mission. And she'd been grateful for every dime, and never let herself judge other people's motivations.

Until now. For some reason, she wasn't willing to let Rick Hunter off so easily, even if refusing his offer hurt her more than it annoyed him.

She took a deep breath. "You can't fix this with money. You're just going to have to deal with the fact that you're disappointing a girl who's already had enough disappointments to last a lifetime."

Something flashed in his eyes, there and gone. "I'm sorry about that, I really am. But I can't believe you wouldn't benefit from a financial contribution. I know nonprofits have been struggling the last couple of years."

That was a hit to her solar plexus.

"Try to get this through your head, Mr. Hunter. *I don't want your money.* But since that's the only topic you're willing to discuss, I might as well go."

"Wait," he said gruffly. "Don't storm out, all right? Just—wait a second."

She'd been on the point of turning away, but now she hesitated. His eyes were on her face, and once again there was something in his expression she couldn't decipher. It held her in place for a moment.

"Look, how about this," he said after a long

pause. "I'll send you a check next week, to give you time to…" He hesitated. "To think things through. I won't hold you to anything you said here today, and I hope you'll accept the donation. Okay? I'm sure you could use the money."

He was making it easy for both of them. She could storm out in self-righteous anger, take a few days to calm down, and deposit his check without having to back down from her lofty position. Not to his face, anyway.

Her jaw felt stiff. "Yes, we could use the money. The Star Foundation is struggling right now. But money is only part of what keeps us going. The heart of what we do is help *people.* When our kids make wishes, they're specific. They're personal. Anyone can donate money, Mr. Hunter. But Julie wants to meet *you.*"

She was trying to reach the man she'd glimpsed so briefly behind the facade. Instead, her words only made him withdraw again.

"I'm sorry."

"But—"

"I don't like hospitals," he said, as if that ended the discussion.

Allison stared at him. "No one likes hospitals. That's why it's so important to help the people who are stuck in them."

"I'm sorry," he said again. His expression was blank and cool.

Had she only imagined seeing a real human being behind that mask? "I'm sorry, too," she said after a moment. "Parents feel so helpless when a child is diagnosed with cancer. Every instinct tells them to protect their kids, and then along comes a situation completely outside their control. That's why it's so frustrating when someone like you could actually *do* something—take some small, positive action to make a difference—only you won't."

Another flash of emotion showed through. "Ms. Landry—"

She wouldn't be drawn in again. "Goodbye, Mr. Hunter."

She left his office without looking back.

In the privacy of the elevator, she took a deep breath. When the doors opened she hurried across the elegant lobby, relieved to step outside again into the fresh air.

She walked quickly, impatient at every crosswalk. Her heart was beating faster than usual. After several blocks she realized she'd gone right past the garage where she'd parked.

She stopped, turned, and went slowly back the way she'd come.

She was supposed to be good with people. It was her job to get them involved, to persuade them they could make a difference.

But she'd failed to make even a dent in Rick Hunter's armor. She'd felt at a disadvantage from the moment she walked into his office, and that wasn't something she was used to.

And she'd ended up with nothing. No visit

for Julie, and no money for the foundation. He'd offered, and she'd turned him down. She'd never refused a donation before.

She slid behind the wheel of her truck and turned the key in the ignition. He'd probably still send a check—he seemed like the persistent type. She'd just have to swallow her pride and accept it.

Pride had no place in her work. Nothing, and certainly not her own ego, could be allowed to get in the way of her mission to help families.

So why had she let Rick Hunter get to her? Why had she taken their encounter so personally? She'd swallowed her pride before—why did this feel so different?

She remembered those moments when she'd seen something underneath his coldness… something like real emotion. Like he really did feel badly about Julie. Like he really did want to help her.

That was the only reason she'd stayed as long

as she did. Once she realized he wasn't going to budge, she should have left. But a part of her had wanted to stay, to see if maybe, just maybe, she could get him to change his mind.

Not just for Julie's sake, but for his, too. It would have been nice to see those two meet— the icy CEO and the irrepressible Julie, who managed to radiate enthusiasm for life even when she was exhausted by cancer treatments. There was no way Rick could meet her and not smile. Not unless the man truly lacked both a soul and a heart.

And somehow, in spite of everything, she didn't think that was the case.

She slammed on her brakes for a red light she'd almost missed, adrenaline prickling her skin.

When the light turned green again she stepped carefully on the gas. It didn't matter why her interaction with Rick Hunter had gotten under her skin. Maybe it was just the accumulated stress of a bad day. But from now on, she'd think of him like any other donor. When his check came, she'd cash it. She'd add him to the foundation's mailing list and send him a thank-you card.

And she'd never have to see him again.

Chapter Two

On the days Rick walked to work, he usually took the most direct route between his condo and his office. Today he made a detour past James Memorial Hospital.

After eighteen years, he could drive past the place without being affected. He saw the hospital through his car window a dozen times a week. But now he stopped in front of the building, looking up at the rows of windows. He still remembered which one had been his mother's.

Fourth floor, third from the left.

He lasted about ten seconds before he walked away. His hands were fisted inside his pockets.

Memories of grief and helplessness were a sick weight in his stomach. During the intervening years he'd built up layers of strength—physical, financial, emotional—all designed to insulate him from ever feeling helpless again.

He'd be a fool to undo any of it, to revisit that pit of emotional hell. The only reason he was even considering it was because of his plan to keep Hunter Hall—the plan he wanted Allison Landry to agree to.

The thought had occurred to him a few minutes after she'd left his office, and he'd dismissed it almost immediately. But then, as the day wore on, he couldn't get the idea out of his head.

He couldn't get her out of his head, either.

Not because he was interested in her. She

was pretty—beautiful, even—but she wasn't remotely his type.

He recalled the sight of her standing in the middle of his polished, expensive office, looking anything but polished and expensive. Allison had been fierce and passionate and focused on her mission. The women he dated were sleek and sophisticated and focused on him— or on landing a rich husband, anyway. And from their five-hundred-dollar hairdos to their manicured toes, they were designed to impress.

Allison didn't give a damn about impressing people. Her personality, her appearance…she was the complete opposite of the women he usually went out with.

And exactly the kind of woman his grandmother wished he would date.

What was it Gran had said? That it wouldn't kill him to date a woman of character for once. That she just wanted to believe he could change his ways.

She wasn't asking for a wedding or an engagement. So maybe, if he was with a woman like Allison for a few months, that would satisfy her.

It would only be for show, of course. Allison wasn't interested in him—that had been pretty damn obvious—and he wasn't interested in her. Which made her perfect, because he had no intention of actually falling for her—or any woman, for that matter. Nothing made a man more helpless than that.

This would be a straightforward business deal, beneficial to both parties.

Provided he could make Allison an offer she couldn't refuse.

When he arrived at the office, Carol was already at her desk. "What are you thinking about, boss? You've got a funny look on your face."

"I was thinking about Allison Landry."

Carol handed him some letters to sign. "I'm

not surprised. That's a young woman who makes an impression."

He scrawled his name on the signature lines. "She made an impression on you, anyway." He handed the letters back. "You liked her, didn't you?"

"I did. The way she charged in here, like David taking on Goliath…when this company was just a start-up, I got to see more people like that. People with passion, you know? Now it's just a parade of business types, corporate suits like you."

He frowned, disliking that characterization more than he would have expected. "You think I'm just a suit?"

"Maybe not," Carol said grudgingly. "But ten more years and that's exactly what you'll be. Of course if you got back to the creative side of things, maybe designed a new game…"

"Games are for children. Why do you think we recruit out of college for that division?"

"You could design for the business software line."

He shook his head. "Give it up, Carol. You know I'm too busy."

"You could hire a couple of VPs to handle some of your corporate responsibilities and free up your time to—"

"Not going to happen."

Carol sighed. "Well, no one can say I didn't try." She glanced down at her message spindle. "Nelson called, by the way. He wants to talk to you about his noncompete agreement."

Rick felt a quick pulse of anger. "He can go to hell. He left us two weeks before product launch and now he's trying to wriggle out of his agreement? Screw that. The next time he calls, refer him to our attorneys."

"I'll give him the message, but you don't always have to be such a hard-ass. Were you like this with Allison Landry? Is that why she blew through here so fast, after she talked to you?"

Rick had started toward his office, but now he paused. "She was upset?"

"She didn't look happy. So I guess that means you're not going to do it, huh?"

"Do what?"

"Visit that girl in the hospital."

Carol knew he avoided hospitals, although she'd never asked him why.

"I'm not planning on it," was all he said now.

He went into his office and shut the door behind him. A few minutes later he was at his computer, reading about the Star Foundation and its young director.

Allison had lost a sister to cancer when she was eighteen. She'd taken a year off before starting college at the University of Iowa, where she eventually majored in business. While she was still in school a small publishing house released a memoir based on the journals Allison had kept during her sister's illness and in the year after her death.

To her own surprise, the memoir had become a bestseller. After she graduated, Allison used the proceeds from her book to start the Star Foundation. The agency provided support to families dealing with childhood cancer and also administered the Wish Upon a Star program, which worked to grant wishes to seriously ill children. In the last five years the foundation had touched the lives of hundreds of families.

Rick leaned back in his chair. She had a pretty impressive resume for a twenty-seven-year-old.

Based on what he'd just read about the agency and the scope of its services, he figured Allison's operating budget was around three million dollars. He could also make a guess as to the financial difficulties she was facing. Nonprofits all around the country were still struggling.

He clicked on an image link, and a photo of Allison popped up on his screen.

Her soft brown bangs and serious expression made her look earnest and idealistic, but the tilt of her chin hinted at the force and determination he'd seen in his office yesterday.

And her bone structure could probably land her a modeling job.

Not a woman who could be easily categorized. When Rick realized he was staring, he closed the internet browser and picked up his phone.

"We had a letter from Telecorp today. They have to cut their annual donation by fifteen percent." Allison sighed, wondering how much more bad news would be coming their way. "I wanted to start paying you this summer. Scott and Beverly, too. Maybe I can still figure a way to—"

"Don't be silly," Rachel said briskly. "I wouldn't let you pay me. What part of volunteer don't you understand?"

"The part where you're getting your MBA next month and will probably be looking for gainful employment."

"If and when that happens, I'll still volunteer on weekends. I love the work we do here, you know that—and I'm not going to abandon you when you need me most. I know we're going through rough times financially, but we'll get through it. And in the meantime, I'm not going to let you or our kids down."

Tears came into Allison's eyes. "You're amazing, you know that?"

The phone rang, and she picked it up absently.

"Star Foundation, Allison speaking."

"Ms. Landry? This is Rick Hunter."

She almost dropped the phone.

"Ms. Landry? Are you there?"

She cleared her throat. "Um…yes. Yes, I'm here."

His rich baritone voice was cool and businesslike. "I'm calling because we didn't end things on the best of terms yesterday, and I'm hoping we can start over."

"Start over?"

"Yes. I have a business proposal for you."

"A business proposal?"

She knew she was repeating everything he said, but she couldn't seem to come up with anything more intelligent.

"Why don't you let me explain over coffee? I've got a busy day, and I'm sure you do too. How about 6:30, at the Starbucks around the corner from your office? Unless there's someplace more convenient for you."

"No, that…would be fine."

"Until then," he said.

"Until then," she echoed.

There was a brief pause. Not sure what else to do, she hung up.

She stared at the phone on her desk, her hand still curled around the receiver. She was meeting Rick Hunter tonight.

So much for never seeing him again.

"Who was that?" Rachel asked curiously.

Allison explained, and Rachel stared at her.

"I don't believe it. You have a date with Rick Hunter!"

"It's not a date. But it's weird, isn't it? What kind of business proposal could he have for me?"

"He doesn't. That's just to camouflage his real interest." Rachel's eyes were sparkling. "He fell madly in love with you at first sight, but sensing your animosity he had to—"

"Will you please join me back here in reality?"

"Reality is overrated. Okay, at least give me

some details. You hardly told me anything yesterday. Is he as sexy in person as he is in that magazine? Just looking at his picture makes me want to burst into song."

Allison's mouth twitched. "Like in a musical?"

Rachel sighed dramatically. "More like an opera. I could do a whole aria about my lust for Rick Hunter. Did you sing while you were in his office?"

"No. I mostly yelled at him for being a selfish jerk. Which he is, by the way. He turned down Julie's wish, and whatever he wants to see me about, I don't think it's to tell me he's changed his mind."

Rachel shook her head. "I tried to tell you before, you're prejudiced. I read about him in that article. His company supports a lot of charities. And he went into the army right after 9/11—that's not selfish, is it?"

Okay, that was surprising. Allison had a soft

spot for soldiers—her brother was overseas right now on his fourth tour of duty.

Of course, military service didn't automatically make Rick Hunter a hero. Not everyone went into the army for noble reasons. Maybe he just wanted to blow things up. He did design all those violent video games, after all.

"You know, I think you're right," she mused aloud.

"I frequently am. About what, specifically?"

"I think I *am* prejudiced. I'm looking for reasons not to like him."

"That's because you're fighting an attraction so powerful you—"

Allison laughed. "Okay, stop. I won't admit to a powerful attraction, but I'll try to keep an open mind when I meet him later. Is that good enough?"

Rachel grinned. "For now."

Rick finished work by five o'clock, which left him time for a quick workout before his

appointment with Allison. He rode the elevator down to the basement, where he'd had a
fitness center installed for his employees.

He was about to start his usual weight circuit
when one of his VPs challenged him to some
one-on-one basketball.

A short but hard fought game left him feeling relaxed and loose. He took a quick shower,
decided to change into jeans and a T-shirt, and
at six-twenty strolled into the Starbucks near
Allison's office.

She wasn't there yet. If she was like nine
women out of ten he knew, she'd be late, of
course. He settled himself at a table in the
back with a black coffee and the *Wall Street
Journal*, but found himself glancing toward
the entrance every couple of minutes.

At six-thirty on the dot, she came through
the door.

He'd been wondering if she would dress any
differently for this second meeting. He was

used to women primping for him, dressing up for him. Hell, he'd been with women who wore makeup to bed.

Not that this was a date, of course. But it wasn't crazy to think that Allison might have put some thought into her appearance before seeing him again.

She gave a nod of recognition when she saw him and threaded her way through the crowd toward his table.

She was wearing jeans and a gray sweatshirt. When she sat down, he could see she wasn't wearing any makeup at all. Not even lip gloss.

Okay, that confirmed it. Allison Landry was not attracted to him.

Which was perfect, he reminded himself. For the kind of arrangement he was looking for, attraction would only be a complication.

"Hello again," he said, laying down his newspaper. "Thanks for agreeing to meet me."

She smiled, and her face was transformed.

Gone was the serious-minded idealist. When she smiled like that she looked sweet, a little playful, and completely charming.

"I have to admit, I'm curious as to what kind of business proposal you have for me."

He hesitated. "Can I get you some coffee first? Or tea?"

"No, thanks."

He hesitated again. The straightforward look in her blue eyes made him feel unsure of himself, something he wasn't used to. "Before I tell you about it, I'd like to apologize for yesterday. We didn't get off on the right foot."

"Maybe not, but we're here to start over, like you said." She rested her forearms on the table and clasped her hands together. "Tell me about your proposal, Mr. Hunter."

"Rick."

"Okay, Rick. And you can call me Allison. Now that we're on a first name basis, will you tell me why I'm here?"

In a negotiation, always lead with strength. He took out the check he'd already signed and slid it across the table.

She frowned at him a second before picking it up.

Her skin was so translucent he could see the flush creeping up from the base of her throat to the roots of her hair. He could practically feel the warmth rising from her skin.

He was caught, fascinated. When was the last time he'd seen such transparent emotion?

She looked up at him.

"This is…" She paused to clear her throat. "This is a check for half a million dollars."

He nodded slowly, his eyes on hers. "Would it help?"

Stupid question. Of course it would help.

"You can't imagine how much," she said, her voice trembling a little. "I was going to spend tomorrow figuring out what programs to cut this year…which services we won't be able to provide. This…" Her chest rose with a quick breath. "This changes everything."

He shouldn't have asked. Now he felt a flicker of guilt, because there were strings attached to that check. For a moment he wished there weren't, that he could bask in the glow of those flushed cheeks and shining eyes and ask nothing in return.

But that's not why he was here. Well and good if their deal helped her out—her foundation did good work and Allison was obviously a good person. But he needed to get something out of this, too. He thought of Hunter Hall and hardened his heart.

"That's one half of the business proposal I was talking about."

She blinked at him. "Right. Yes. Of course." She shook her head, smiling ruefully. "I'm sorry if I got carried away. The sight of all those zeros was a little overwhelming."

He watched her rein in her emotions. And

even though he knew it would be easier to negotiate if they were both in business mode, a part of him missed the stars that had been in her eyes a moment ago.

She laid the check back down on the table. "Well, you certainly have my attention. I'd like to accept this donation if it's possible. So what do you need in return?"

"I need a woman like you." He paused. "Specifically, I need people to believe you and I are a couple. If you'll pretend to date me for three months, that check is yours."

Silence.

Allison stared at him, and he looked back at her steadily. Then she cocked her head to the side, as if she wasn't sure she'd heard right.

"You want me to…pretend to date you?"

"Yes."

Another silence. "Okay, I'm waiting for the punch line. Because this is a joke, right?"

"No. It's a straightforward business proposition."

She stared at him for another minute. Then she sat slowly back in her chair, her eyes still on his.

"I'm going to need some backstory here," she said at last. "I read last month's *People*, and I find it very hard to believe that Rick Hunter, Playboy of the Midwest, needs to pay five hundred thousand dollars for a fake girlfriend."

Damn that magazine. "That article is the reason I'm asking you to do this. My grandmother has never liked the women I date, and after she read that piece…well, let's just say she wasn't happy. And because of that, I'm going to lose something. Something that's important to me."

Allison frowned. "And pretending to date me is going to fix that somehow?"

"That's the idea." He remembered Gran's

exact words. "My grandmother wants me to date a woman of character. The minute I met you, I knew you fit the bill. So I'm proposing a business deal. An arrangement that would benefit us both."

For someone who could be so transparent with her emotions, Allison could also put on a pretty good poker face. "What is it that you want? That you don't want to lose?"

An image of Hunter Hall flashed into his mind. "A house."

She raised an eyebrow. "I think you can afford to buy your own house."

That made him smile. "Yeah, but not this one. It's been in the family for more than a hundred years. Hunter Hall, it's called."

"And would your grandmother really sell your family estate? Just because she doesn't like the women in your life?"

He hadn't planned on going into this much detail. "Not exactly. She's moving to the city this summer, and she was going to transfer ownership of Hunter Hall to me. But now she's talking about giving the house to someone else—a second cousin. She wants a family to live in Hunter Hall. My cousin is married, and wants to have kids. So he says, anyway."

"And you don't want that? A family, I mean?"

His jaw tightened. He wasn't husband or father material, but that wasn't something he'd be discussing with Allison. "I'm happy as a bachelor and I intend to stay that way. Which is why I date…the women I date."

"I see." She was studying him thoughtfully, and her level, blue-eyed gaze was disconcerting.

She glanced down at the check for a moment, and then back up at him. "Look, I won't lie to you. I'd love to accept this donation. But I don't think—"

She was going to say no. He interrupted her

before she could finish. "It's just a few dinners and parties, Allison. What's the big deal?"

"I'm not the only woman of character in Iowa. Couldn't you—"

"You're not attracted to me."

She blinked. "What?"

"I said, you're not attracted to me. That's why you're perfect."

She frowned at him. "How do you know?"

He could have told her his lip gloss theory of female behavior, but it wasn't just that. He'd had close to twenty years of dating experience; he knew when a woman was attracted to him.

"It's true, isn't it? And I'm not attracted to you."

In actual point of fact, the more time he spent with her, the more attracted he felt. It was the reverse of what usually happened when he met a beautiful woman. Usually his attraction kicked off with a bang and went downhill from there.

But since he had no interest in dating her for real, it didn't seem to matter—and he knew Allison would be more comfortable with the lie.

"Nothing personal," he added when she raised her eyebrows, although she didn't look insulted. "You're just not my type. And that's why this plan will work. I get Hunter Hall, your foundation gets half a million dollars— and when it's all over, no one gets hurt."

He leaned across the table toward her. "Say yes, Allison."

The brief flash of intensity in his green eyes caught her off guard. It was like a weapon he could unleash without warning. Rick Hunter, she suspected, very seldom asked for anything he didn't get.

She looked down at his check, that small rectangle of paper that for just a moment had made her so happy.

The money would mean so much to the foundation…would mean so much to the families she supported. But the fact was, she hadn't been in a relationship since high school. The thought of changing that now—even if it was in name only—sent a nervous tremor through her.

"Listen…Rick." She cleared her throat. "I don't…"

He sat back again, the expression in his eyes more reserved now. "You're seeing someone."

The simplest thing would be to say yes. But Allison was naturally honest, and she found herself shaking her head. "No, I'm not seeing anyone. But—"

"But what?" That persuasive tone was back, the one she was sure served him well in business and his personal life.

She took a deep breath. "I don't date. You like your life the way it is? I like mine, too. You stay single by dating women you won't get serious with. I stay single by not dating at all. At this point, anyway."

He looked genuinely surprised. "When's the last time you were in a relationship?"

She didn't want to tell him it had been almost ten years. He wouldn't understand…not unless she told him things she'd never told her own mother. Things she'd never told a living soul.

"It's been a while," she said evasively.

His gaze moved over her face and down her torso, and then back up to her face. She was wearing a bulky gray sweatshirt, so it wasn't like he was getting an eyeful, but she could feel her face turn red at his appraisal.

"I have to admit, I'm surprised. But if you're not seeing anyone, I don't see the problem."

She started to get impatient. "The problem is, everyone in my life knows I don't date. They don't understand it, but they accept it. If I start seeing someone out of the blue they'll go nuts. They'll want to meet you. My family especially. I have an older brother and sister and none of us are married yet, and my parents really want grandchildren. If my mom gets the idea that I'm seeing someone, she'll start planning a wedding. It'll be awful."

She took a breath. "And there's no way they wouldn't find out. You're news. If we start going out, it'll be in all the local papers."

"My grandmother's the only one who needs to think we're romantically involved," he said after a moment. "You can tell your friends and family whatever you want. Tell them we're going out as friends and that the media's making more of it than it is."

He leaned forward, his biceps bunching as he rested his forearms on the table. His black T-shirt stretched across his broad shoulders.

"Say you'll do it." His voice was forceful and persuasive at the same time, backed up by that intense gaze and a quick, flashing smile.

Allison felt her palms getting sweaty. A very

inelegant reaction, one the women Rick Hunter dated probably never experienced.

He was persuasive, all right. And confident, like there was no doubt he'd get his way in the end.

Allison rubbed her palms on her denim-clad thighs and scooted her chair back a few inches, putting a little distance between them. She'd seen this kind of confidence before—plenty of times, in fact. It had been a defining characteristic of a lot of the rich kids she'd gone to high school with. The boys especially, and one in particular. Paul had been so confident it had been impossible to imagine him ever failing to get something he wanted.

She folded her arms across her chest. "I'm sorry, but I'm not your solution here."

He looked surprised. "You won't do it?"

"Don't look so shocked. You're obviously used to people falling all over themselves to give you whatever you want, but—"

Now he was frowning. "I don't expect people to fall all over me."

She rolled her eyes. "Oh, please. I bet no one ever says no to you. Come on, admit it. Don't you usually get your way? Maybe always?"

He folded his arms, like her. "No."

"You grew up rich, didn't you? I can spot the attitude a mile off. The silver spoon crowd—you're all alike. You think because you—"

"Hey! Stop doing that."

His voice was sharp enough that she actually did. "Stop doing what?" she asked.

"Stop making assumptions. Stop judging me because I have money. I'm sorry if that offends you—"

"That's not what offends me. It's your obvious belief that everything—and everyone—should just fall in your lap."

He leaned forward again. "I don't think that. I've never thought that. Believe me, I could give you a long list of things I've wanted in my life that I didn't get."

She frowned at him. "You ooze confidence. It practically…drips off you."

He shook his head. "I'm not going to apologize for being confident. I am confident. But not because I have money, in spite of what you obviously believe. I'm confident because I believe in myself. Don't you believe in yourself?"

Of course she did. As far as work went, anyway. As for personal stuff…

Irrelevant, Allison decided. She shrugged impatiently. "I suppose. Anyway, we got off track with the—"

"You got off track, as I recall. With your prejudice against the wealthy."

"I'm not prejudiced."

"What I don't get is how you can run a charitable foundation. Aren't rich people kind of your bread and butter? How do you manage to hide the fact that you despise them when you're asking for donations?"

She flushed. "That's a terrible thing to say. For one thing, it's not only the wealthy who contribute to charities. And for another, I don't hate rich people. I'm incredibly grateful to anyone who donates their money—or their time—to the Star Foundation. Especially when they do it because they want to, and not because they expect something in return."

His jaw tightened. "Unlike me, right? Is that what you wanted to hear? Yes, I'm selfish. No, I don't give without expecting something back. I'm sorry I don't meet your high standards for human behavior, or fit into your perfect little world where everyone acts like a saint. But here's a reality flash for you."

He stabbed a forefinger on the table in front of her. "Charities all over the country are struggling right now, and yours is no exception. You can keep on looking down your nose at me, and let your foundation suffer—or you can admit you need my money and take it. How many of the families you pretend to care so much about will be hurt if you turn me down?"

He leaned back again. "Sounds pretty damn selfish to me."

She was so mad her hands were shaking. But the worst part was, she knew he was right.

If she turned down his donation, she'd have to cut programs and services. The reality of that stared her in the face.

Looking across the table at him, seeing the coldness that had come into his expression, Allison felt a sudden wave of recklessness.

Why shouldn't she accept his offer? They'd go out to a few overpriced restaurants and have a few stilted conversations. Why had the idea of that made her feel so nervous, so awkward and unsure of herself? Right now, she didn't feel awkward at all. The anger flowing in her veins made her feel like she could do anything.

So yes, she'd take his money. With a donation this big, she might be able to add some services this year. Expand her existing programs. Reach more families.

And she'd get something else from him, too.

"I'll do it."

He blinked at her in surprise. "What?"

"I accept your proposal."

"You do?"

"On one condition." She leaned forward, schooling her features into what she hoped was an implacable expression. "You'll visit Julie in the hospital this Saturday."

To drop her eyes at this point would be a sign of weakness, so she held his gaze as his eyes narrowed and his dark brows slanted together.

After a minute he started to drum the fingers of one hand against the table. When he real-

ized what he was doing he curled that hand
into a fist.

"What if I say no?"

She shrugged. "You'll have to find another
woman of character who's not attracted to you.
It won't be that hard. From where I sit, those
two qualities seem to go together naturally."

Another minute of silence. Then his fisted
hand relaxed, and he leaned back in his chair.

"I should have realized you were capable
of driving a hard bargain. You don't give up
easily, do you?"

"The families I work with don't give up. I
hold myself to the same standard." She took a
quick breath. "So do we have a deal, or not?"

His eyes didn't leave hers. "We have a deal,"
he said.

A deal.

Half a million dollars for the foundation, and
Julie's wish granted.

And a date with one of *People* magazine's

Most Eligible Bachelors. Several dates, actually. A few months worth of dates.

She felt a little dizzy. "Okay, then." She took another breath. "I'm sure you've got better things to do than sit here with me all night." She took out her wallet and tucked his check carefully inside. Her hands shook a little. "When can I deposit this?" she asked. "Do you want me to wait until after I've honored my side of the bargain?"

He shook his head. "No, I trust you. You're a woman of character, remember?"

He was actually smiling a little, and she smiled back reluctantly. "I'll let Julie know you'll be coming by on Saturday."

If he'd been anyone but a powerful CEO, she would have said a look of panic came into his eyes. "I assumed you'd be there, too. Won't you be there?"

He was probably one of those single men who weren't comfortable around kids. Was that the reason he'd been so reluctant to do this?

She sighed. "I can be there if you want. Two o'clock, at the hospital?"

Some of the tension went out of his expression. "Yes, fine. And we'll go to dinner that night."

It was Allison's turn to feel a pang of anxiety.

"Now, can I drop you somewhere?"

He rose to his feet and offered her a hand. Allison extended her own, a little hesitantly, and it was enveloped in a strong, warm grip as he helped her up. She took a step back as she pulled her hand away, tingles radiating from her palm and blood rushing to her cheeks.

"I'm all set. But thanks."

He was just a foot or so away. She had to tilt her head back to look at him.

She backed away another step. "Well…good night."

Her heart racing, she turned away, moving quickly through the crowd to get to the door. She pushed it open and stood outside for a moment, taking in a big gulp of cool evening air.

She'd made a deal with Rick Hunter. A straightforward business arrangement, as he called it.

Sure it was straightforward—to him. As for her…well, straightforward wasn't the word she'd use to describe her mental state at the moment.

She took another breath. This was for her foundation. She needed to think about the families she could help with Rick's money—not Rick himself, with his black hair and intense green eyes and well-muscled body.

She wouldn't think about his coldness, either…or the few times something else had broken through, just for a moment.

He thought she wasn't attracted to him.

She prayed he'd still believe that when their deal expired. Because she didn't like him, and she didn't want to be attracted to him.

And she definitely didn't want him to know that she was.

Chapter Three

Rick had convinced himself it wouldn't be so bad. An hour, maybe two at the most.

But right now, staring up at the marble facade of James Memorial Hospital, he couldn't make his feet take the steps that would lead him inside that building.

"Rick?"

He turned, and Allison was there beside him.

She looked like a breath of fresh air in a long-sleeved cotton blouse, pale yellow with lavender stripes. Faded jeans showed off her slender legs. Her silky short hair was the perfect frame for her face, with her wide cheekbones and pointed chin and serious blue eyes. In the April sunlight, strands of gold made the chestnut brown shimmer. He wondered why he'd always preferred long hair on women.

"Hello," he said.

Allison was frowning. "Are you all right? You look like you're feeling sick. Should we reschedule?"

He shook his head. He was damned if he was going to give in to weakness like this—especially in front of Allison. "I'm fine," he lied. "Went out with some friends last night, with an emphasis on Southern Comfort. I guess I'm still feeling the effects." That was true—except about feeling the effects. He might be thirty-five but he could hold his liquor like he was twenty-one.

"Well…if you're sure." She started toward the revolving glass doors, and he forced himself to follow her. Focus on Allison, he told himself. She looked so…reassuring, somehow. Sweet and fresh and warm.

He made it all the way across the lobby before he had to stop again. They were right in front of the gift shop. In spite of everything he could do, memories of the last time he'd visited this place flooded through him.

He'd gotten flowers for his mother the day before she died. For years afterward, the scent of flowers had made him sick.

"Rick! Are you all right?"

He hated that Allison was seeing him like this. He hated that he couldn't control himself better. He should be able to control himself. He was a successful man at the height of his career.

And right now, he might as well be seventeen again. It felt like everything he'd worked for since then had been stripped away.

"Rick, you're scaring me. You have to tell me what's wrong."

"I just…need a second."

He walked a few paces to a waiting area and sat down on a hard plastic chair. He leaned forward, resting his elbows on his knees and looking down at the floor tiles. He was aware that Allison had sat down next to him, but he was focusing all his attention on his breathing, on trying to slow his heart rate, on trying to be himself again. Calm and in control.

"I'm sorry," he said after a few minutes, when he could look at her again. He thought of a dozen lies he could tell, all believable, but each and every one of them stuck in his throat.

"My mother died of cancer," he said abruptly. His voice sounded rough and strange to his own ears. "In this hospital, eighteen years ago. I haven't been back here since. I haven't been in any hospital since."

He'd never told anyone that before. He hadn't

talked about his mother since the day she died. And why the hell should he? It wasn't anybody's damn business—including Allison's. He could feel his face flushing, like a boy's. A flicker of anger made his jaw tighten.

"I'm sorry," she said, laying a hand on his arm. "You should have told me. We don't have to stay. Let's leave now, all right?"

The anger died. How could he be angry with Allison? Her hand on his arm was so gentle, and her eyes conveyed compassion without the pity he would have resented.

"No," he said, straightening up in his chair. He took a deep breath. "I'm okay. And I want to do this." He looked down at her. "Your sister died of cancer, didn't she? I read it in your bio. And I don't see you running away from hospitals. Or people with cancer."

She shook her head, rejecting the comparison. "If there's one thing I've learned in the last ten years, it's that people react differently to grief. I responded by—well, by making cancer my mission. That was what I needed to do, to get through it. You had a different reaction. But you shouldn't judge yourself for the way you responded to your loss. And you shouldn't force yourself to do this right now if you're not ready for it. I can tell Julie…"

"No. I want to see her. And I won't be…like this."

"It's okay if you are. These kids don't need people to put on happy faces like clown makeup. It's good to be positive, but it's even better to be real. To be whoever you are. Kids are perceptive—they know when you're lying to them. Do you know what I mean?"

"Yes," he said. He took a deep breath. "Okay, then. Let's go."

Allison could feel the tension coursing through him as they rode the elevator to the fifth floor and stepped out into the pediatric ward.

Rick hadn't turned down Julie's wish because he was selfish. He'd turned it down because he'd known how hard it would be to come back here. To revisit his loss.

She'd broken one of her cardinal rules— never to judge someone without knowing them. Her work put her in a position to see people at their worst as well as their best, and because of that, she always tried to give people the benefit of the doubt. Always, no matter what the circumstances. Human beings were complex, and she never wanted to take shortcuts through that complexity, to define people based on superficialities.

So why had she been so quick to judge Rick?

She remembered how he'd looked down in the lobby, like a boy confronted with an uncomfortable emotion—grief or anger or shame. She wondered how he'd react when he saw Julie. The young girl certainly looked like a cancer patient, with her thin, pale face and the scarf she wore to hide her baldness.

When they entered her room Julie was staring at the TV monitor in front of her with fixed intensity, holding a video game controller in her hand and manipulating buttons so fast Allison couldn't follow the motions. She seemed completely unaware of her surroundings. Allison and Rick came up to her bedside and she didn't even register their presence.

Allison glanced over at Rick, and was glad to see that he looked better. He was watching what Julie was doing, and Allison remembered with a sudden shock that he had actually designed this game. She looked at the monitor they were both studying and saw several characters, all more or less medieval looking, with swords and spears and bows, facing down forty or fifty unpleasant looking lizard-like creatures who also were holding swords.

Julie gave a cry of frustration as one of the characters on screen—a tall, blond man in chain mail—took an arrow in the neck and fell writhing to the ground.

"Quick," Rick said, grabbing the controls from Julie and doing something Allison couldn't follow. "That kind of armor has a one-time healing spell woven into it. Hardly anyone under level forty knows about it, but—"

Before their eyes Julie's character sat up, pulled the arrow out of his miraculously healed flesh, and leapt to his feet. He uttered a bloodcurdling battle cry and hurled himself back into the fray.

Rick paused the game and handed the controls back to Julie. "Sorry," he said. "I get carried away sometimes. My name is—"

"I know who you are," Julie said. Her voice was hushed, her eyes luminous as she stared at him.

Allison hid her smile. "Julie, this is Richard Hunter. Rick, this is Julie Pratt."

"Hi, Julie," Rick said, smiling as he held out his hand. Julie looked like she was in the presence of royalty, or at least Taylor Lautner, as she shook it.

"Is Eric your favorite?" Rick was asking, grabbing a chair and sitting down by Julie's bed.

"Uh-huh," Julie said. "I like that he can use magic but he's also a warrior. You know? And he has such a tragic past."

"He's definitely the most complex character," Rick agreed. "Do you want to play two-person? I could take Teska or Unthas if you'd like."

Julie made a kind of gurgling sound that Allison thought was probably an affirmative. Rick must have interpreted it the same way, because he took a spare controller from the shelf below the monitor and settled back into his chair with a look on his face that mirrored Julie's as the two of them started pushing buttons.

Allison pulled up a chair herself and sat quietly, fascinated by the instant bond created by this game. Rick and Julie were talking to each other about battle tactics, about something called the Gem of Fanor, and about the mind games their characters had to endure in the Labyrinth of Dreams, which could, apparently, reveal the characters' deepest motivations and desires but could also deceive and betray. The characters all seemed to have complicated backstories that tied into their quests, which both Rick and Julie knew inside and out.

This was a different Rick Hunter than the man she'd met two days ago. He'd been hit by a painful memory today—a memory that had the power to get past his defenses. He'd faced it, and now it was as if he'd forgotten to put his armor back on. He was talking and laughing with Julie as if they were both sixteen.

Allison cleared her throat. "It looks like you two are busy, so I'm going to pay a few visits. See you in a bit, okay?"

Julie didn't even hear her, but Rick gave her a quick grin before turning back to the young girl who looked like she'd been given the best gift of her life.

Allison visited several patients before going back to check on Rick and Julie. They were still talking about the game, although the TV was off now. Julie was sitting straight up in bed and chatting a mile a minute, like any normal teenage girl. Allison was so happy to see her like that it was a few minutes before she paid any attention to what they were saying.

"I've made it inside a few times, but only to the front hallway. The spell always ends so fast. A friend of mine made it into the library once, and he actually found the Book of Hadram before the magic sent him back to the forest. He brought the book with him, too, and the spells and maps in there got him up to the seventeenth level. I suppose I shouldn't ask you how to stay in the house longer, right? I mean, I should probably figure it out for myself. I know it's a combination of different magics, but of course the higher level players are all cagey about the secrets they've figured out. I'd love to have time to explore the whole house, you know? Since Rick—I mean, oh my gosh, *you*—put all kinds of cool stuff in there. Plus I've heard it's really beautiful inside. Is it true that it's based on your own house?"

"Not mine," Rick corrected. "It's based on Hunter Hall, which belongs to my grandmother. I spent some time there as a kid."

That was the house Rick had talked about at the coffee shop…the house his grandmother was going to give to someone else.

"Can I see it?" Allison asked suddenly,

causing Rick and Julie to notice that she was in the doorway for the first time.

"Hi," Rick said, standing up to offer her his chair.

"Does this mean he has to go?" Julie asked mournfully, and Allison shook her head. "Not at all—unless you have to be somewhere?" she asked Rick belatedly. Not everyone had the appetite for kid conversation that she did.

"Nope," he said, causing Julie to smile like a sunrise.

"So, can I see this house you were talking about?" Allison asked again, and Julie moved over on the bed so she could sit beside her, while Rick sat back down on the chair.

"Here," Julie said, turning the TV back on and clicking the video controls until a picture of a three story stone mansion filled the screen. "That's the magician's house. If you can figure out how to find it, and then how to get through the magic barrier, and then figure out how to stay there longer than a minute or two, there's amazing stuff hidden all around that will help you advance in the game."

"It's beautiful," Allison said, noting the gorgeous detail that had been lavished on every inch: the intricate carving and tracery around the windows and arches, gables and turrets. "Did you really design that?" she asked, turning to Rick. She heard the admiration in her voice and hoped she wasn't starting to sound like Julie.

"I designed the game, but the house, like I said, is based on Hunter Hall. So I had something real to work from."

Julie asked a question then, something about the game that went over her head. As Rick answered her in technical terms that also went over her head, Allison leaned back against Julie's bed pillows and studied the house on the screen.

After a minute she looked at Rick, laughing

and relaxed as he talked about gaming strategies to someone who bore no resemblance, at this moment, to a girl whose body and life had been ravaged by cancer.

He was wearing a tan button-down shirt and a pair of faded jeans that emphasized how long and hard-muscled his legs were. His boots were as well-worn as the jeans, and she had a good view of them as he leaned back in his chair, his legs stretched out in front of him, one ankle hooked over the other.

Watching him like this was like watching a lion recline in the sun. There was a sense of power at rest, of coiled strength in every muscle—and a keen intelligence, too, that could be just as overwhelming as physical force.

Rick Hunter was the last person in the world you could imagine feeling sorry for. He was the picture of male success—money, good looks, power and prestige. How did that jibe with the man she'd glimpsed down in the lobby, who eighteen years later still found his mother's death almost too painful to face? And how did it jibe with the house he'd created in his game, a house like a holy grail—a source of magic that was practically out of reach, that most players could only wish for and never attain?

Allison wasn't sure. But she knew that there was more to Rick Hunter than met the eye, and that she'd judged him without knowing him, just like he'd said.

A few minutes later a nurse came in, glancing ostentatiously at the clock, and Rick and Allison both rose to their feet.

"I wish you didn't have to go," Julie said wistfully, holding her arm out for the blood pressure cuff. "I don't suppose…I mean…you wouldn't want to come again, would you?"

"Sure I would," Rick said, and Allison was positive she'd never seen any human being radiate as much pure happiness as Julie did in that moment.

"You made her day," Allison told him in the elevator. "What am I saying? You made her century."

Rick shook his head. "I think I had more fun than she did. It's been a long, long time since I actually played a video game. And Julie's a great kid."

The elevator doors opened and they walked back through the lobby. Rick let her precede him through the revolving doors and they stepped outside, into the bright sunshine and fitful spring breeze.

Rick turned to face her. "I'm glad you made me do this. I'm glad I didn't miss out on meeting Julie."

"I'm glad, too."

He cleared his throat. "So…dinner tonight. I'll pick you up around seven, okay?"

Allison felt a clench of uneasiness. It had

been easier to think about going through with these fake dates when she'd felt indifferent to Rick, or even hostile toward him. But today she'd seen the man behind the facade, and a part of her wanted to see more.

Foolish thought. Their date tonight wasn't real: it was a business arrangement. As far as Rick Hunter was concerned, she was just a means to an end.

She took a breath. "Seven is fine. And thanks again for what you did today. For Julie."

She felt a little better as she remembered the radiant smile that had lit up the girl's face. In the grand scheme of things, any awkwardness or uncertainty she might feel tonight was a small price to pay for that. "You granted her wish," she said now. "You did a good thing."

He frowned. "I never thought I'd be in the wish-granting business. I gave up on wishes a long time ago."

That sounded more like the CEO she'd met

in his office, and the man she'd sat across from at Starbucks. Rick was retreating back into his familiar persona, and a part of her resisted the change.

"I don't believe anyone can give up on wishes. Not completely. Don't you still wish for Hunter Hall? Isn't that why you're here today?"

He shrugged. His dark hair fell across his forehead, giving him a boyish look that contrasted with his cool expression. "I don't know if it qualifies as a wish. But yes, I want Hunter Hall. It's my one weakness."

She tilted her head as she looked up at him. "So if your plan works, you won't have any weaknesses at all?"

He was quiet for a moment, looking down at her. Then he started to smile. "Are you making fun of me?"

The smile gave her another glimpse of the man she'd seen with Julie…the man she felt so drawn to. "Not on purpose," she said. That time there was definitely a teasing tone in her voice, but his smile had reached his eyes, warming them, and he didn't seem to mind.

She shifted her weight from one foot to the other. "Well…goodbye, Rick. I'll see you in a few hours."

He nodded. "I made reservations at Ambrosia. The food is great, and there's usually at least one gossip columnist at the bar. The sooner we get our picture in the paper, the better."

Their picture in the paper.

In the eyes of the world, she would be dating Rick Hunter. A man who intrigued and frustrated her by turns, a man who'd been completely up-front about his lack of interest in her—and who believed she wasn't interested in him.

She wished it were true. She wished she could approach this whole deal as coolly and impersonally as he did, with no emotion involved.

If she hadn't caught a glimpse of the warmth and vulnerability behind his armor, maybe she could.

But it was too late for that.

Chapter Four

A few hours later Allison stood in front of her closet, trying to decide what to wear.

She'd been at Rachel's a few weeks ago when her friend was getting ready for a date. Rachel had ended up with outfits strewn all over her bedroom before she'd finally picked one. Then she'd applied her makeup with more than her usual care, spent twenty minutes making her golden hair look like she hadn't done a thing to it, and spritzed on the barest hint of a spicy perfume.

She'd been struck by the look on Rachel's face during this flurry of activity. Her excitement and anticipation had built until she announced she was ready, her eyes sparkling as she gave herself one last look in the mirror.

Remembering that evening now, Allison felt a twinge of jealousy. Not over Rachel's date, whose face she couldn't even recall, but over her uncomplicated pleasure in the dating process itself. While she hadn't been out with a man in over a year, she'd been single for much longer than that.

Ten years. It had been ten years since the night she'd broken up with Paul.

The night she'd lied about to everyone, including her own family.

A horseback riding accident—that's what she told them. How could she tell them the truth? That her boyfriend had beaten her so badly she'd spent the night in the hospital with a fractured collarbone, a broken wrist and two broken ribs?

Megan was in the cancer ward upstairs. Allison had told her parents to go back there, that she was fine, that she needed to sleep. She didn't think she'd fooled the social worker who'd paid her a visit, but she was eighteen and there wasn't much the woman could do without her cooperation.

She'd been so sure it was the right thing to do. Megan was dying, and it took every bit of her parents' strength and courage just to keep from falling apart. She couldn't add to the burden they were already carrying.

That was her reason in the beginning. But after a while, the secret became a part of her. Her wounds had closed over, and she saw no point in reopening them. She didn't want anyone to feel sorry for her or see her as a victim, and she didn't want to see herself that way, either.

But keeping silent had carried a price. She'd found that out a few years later, when she decided she was ready to start dating again. The guy who'd asked her out was nice enough, but she'd felt so tense and skittish when she was out with him that she'd never returned his calls after that first night.

The same thing happened a year or so later, and a year or so after that.

Finally she'd sworn off dating for good. Not just because of her own baggage, but so she could focus on her work.

Her work was her passion. Why should she waste her time looking for romance? What had that empty dream ever gotten her? She'd believed she was in love with Paul, and she'd wasted time and energy and emotion on him when she hadn't had any to spare. Every minute she'd spent with him was time she hadn't spent with Megan—time she'd never get back.

She watched her friends fall in and out of love, and even in and out of marriages, and she didn't want that for herself. Once in a while a man caught her eye, but the flare of attraction was never strong enough to make her risk her heart. She didn't want to waste time on something that wasn't real. Her family was real, and her work was real, and that was enough.

That's what she told herself, anyway. Just like she told herself she could reverse her no-dating policy anytime she wanted to. Anytime she felt ready.

And now, here she was—not ready at all. Not the slightest bit ready. But she was going on this date anyway, because she'd made a deal to keep her foundation alive, and she couldn't back out of it now.

Even though that deal would put her at a candlelit table with Rick Hunter in less than an hour.

It wasn't real, she reminded herself. And

in case she was in any danger of forgetting that, all she had to do was open that issue of *People* and look at the photos of all the women Rick had been linked with over the years—the women he'd actually been attracted to.

She ran both hands through her hair. Even if she weren't carrying around old baggage she'd never be rid of, how could this night be anything but awkward? She was attracted to Rick—along with every woman who'd ever seen him—but he was only going out with her because he wanted something from his grandmother, and because she was the means to an end.

Not exactly the recipe for a magical evening.

She shook her head sharply. At least she could stop wondering what to wear tonight, like some starry-eyed teenager getting ready for a school dance. For one thing, she wasn't capable of feeling like that anymore—if she ever had been. And for another, Rick had made it clear he wasn't attracted to her, that she was perfect for this arrangement *because* he wasn't attracted to her.

So, fine. She knew she wasn't anything like the women he usually dated, and she certainly wasn't planning to compete with them. So what did it matter what she wore?

She'd treat tonight like a dinner with a hospital executive or prospective donor. She reached toward the "business formal" end of her closet and grabbed something at random.

"Am I early?" Rick asked when she buzzed him up to her apartment. He stood in her doorway looking ridiculously handsome, and her stomach did a little flip.

She didn't know much about men's clothes, but she knew the suit Rick wore must have been tailored for his broad shoulders, and that the gunmetal gray jacket, crisp white shirt and emerald paisley tie were perfectly chosen to set off his coal black hair and intense green eyes.

His jaw was smooth, with no shadow of stubble. She also caught a hint of aftershave—something subtle and expensive, like cedar wood and mountain air.

He was so debonair, so flawless, so confident. She'd seen another side of him at the hospital today, but that hint of vulnerability was gone now. She doubted she'd get a glimpse behind the armor tonight.

Not that it mattered. She wasn't going to fall at his feet. He might be the best-looking man who had ever or would ever stand in her doorway, but she wasn't an idiot, and she had her pride.

"No, you're not early."

He glanced down at her dark slacks, high-necked blouse, and plain tailored suit jacket. "It looks like you just came back from a meeting. If you still need to change I could—"

"This is what I'm wearing," she said firmly.

She felt perversely glad that she hadn't tried to dress the way most women would for a night out, especially with a man like Rick Hunter. She might be pretending to date him, but she didn't have to pretend to be someone she wasn't.

"Do you have a problem with that?" she added.

Her words and her tone were a little belligerent, but he just shook his head. "Not at all." He held out a bouquet of flowers she hadn't even noticed he was carrying. "For you."

"What are those for?" she asked suspiciously.

He raised an eyebrow, and she realized how ungracious her words were a second after they came out of her mouth.

"Sorry," she said quickly. "It's just…no one's here to see, and we're only dating for show."

She reached out to accept the bouquet, and her fingers brushed against his. It was only the briefest contact, but she felt a sudden rush of vertigo, as though she were looking over the edge of a cliff.

"These aren't for our date," he said. "They're to thank you for today. Like I said, I really enjoyed meeting Julie—and I would have missed out on that experience if you weren't such a tough negotiator."

He smiled at her, and she felt that dizzying rush again.

"Well…thanks. I'll go put these in water." She took a step or two toward the kitchen before she paused and looked back at the man still standing in her doorway. "Would you like to come in for a minute?" she asked belatedly.

"Sure," he said, stepping across the threshold into her small apartment.

He made it seem even smaller. "I'll be right back," she said, disappearing quickly into the kitchen.

She took a deep breath before taking a vase out of a cupboard and setting it under the faucet to fill.

There was no reason to feel so tense. She'd been comfortable enough with Rick at the hospital today. She just had to think of him as a business associate—which, in fact, he was. She snipped the ends off the stems and arranged the flowers in water.

She carried the vase into the living room and set it on the coffee table. Rick was over by her DVD shelves, looking at the titles.

"You like old movies."

She nodded. "I love them. I host a classic movie night once a month, for a group of friends."

"You've got a great collection," he said, crossing the room toward her. "And I like the way you've decorated. Your apartment feels like you…warm and personal."

"Thanks," she said. "I've been here almost five years, so I've had plenty of time to settle in."

She took a deep breath. Maybe this wouldn't be so hard after all.

Then he came up to her and offered his arm. "Shall we?"

And just like that, her palms were sweating.

It would help if he wasn't so blatantly masculine. He made her feel all feminine and fluttery—and she didn't do fluttery. She really, really didn't.

"Allison? Are you ready to go?"

"Yes," she said quickly. "Sorry." She rubbed her hand on her pants before placing it in the crook of his arm. "I told you I haven't done this in a while, right?"

"You did. How long is a while?"

He led her to the door, and she snagged her purse on the way. "It's been almost ten years since I was in a relationship."

He stared at her. "How long since you were on a date?" he asked as she pulled the door closed behind them. She'd used that opportunity to drop his arm, but now he put a hand on her lower back to guide her toward the elevator.

Such a casual gesture, for him—but his touch felt like an electric shock. Sensation flooded through her, lingering in odd corners of her body…the insides of her elbows and the beds of her fingernails and the soles of her feet.

"More than a year," she said after a moment, praying her voice sounded normal.

In the elevator he dropped his hand. "That's hard to believe," he said, his eyes finding hers in the reflective surface of the elevator doors. He held her gaze as they rode down, and even though they were side by side, not touching at all, looking at him this way felt strangely intimate.

Then the elevator doors opened, and they

stepped out into the foyer. Once outside she took a quick, deep breath, grateful for the spring chill in the night air.

The "beep beep" of a car unlocking came from nearby. Rick led her to a sleek black Porsche, opening the passenger-side door and standing back to allow her to step inside the leather scented interior. She sank down into the low seat as Rick came around to the driver's side. A moment later, the car purred to life. Rick glanced in the rearview mirror and pulled away from the curb.

She tried not to be too obvious about studying his profile as they drove. Conversation was minimal—she was too nervous for chitchat.

The restaurant wasn't far away. They pulled up in front of a red awning before she knew it, and Rick turned his head to look at her. Her heart thumped as she looked quickly away. Did he know she'd been staring?

"Have you been to Ambrosia before?"

"No," she said as the valet opened her door and helped her out. Rick tossed him the keys and joined her, letting her precede him through the heavy oak doors held open by an employee. The interior of the restaurant was lovely, with dark wood paneling, red velvet chairs, and candlelit tables creating an atmosphere of quiet elegance.

"The food is wonderful," he told her as they were led through the oak-paneled bar to a corner table in the dining room. "The wine list, too," he added as the maître d' pulled out Allison's chair for her. She felt awkward as she sat, not sure how much weight to put on the chair as he pushed it forward.

The silence that settled over the table felt awkward, too.

"Allison?" Rick asked as she took a quick sip of her water and choked. She coughed for a few seconds, feeling like an idiot. After a minute she was breathing normally again.

"What?" she asked, sounding as ungracious as she had at her apartment.

He sat back in his chair, studying her. "You're reneging on our deal."

She stared at him. "No, I'm not. I'm here, aren't I?"

"No one's going to believe you're here on a date. You look like you're next in line for the guillotine."

She bit her lip. What could she say to that? He was right.

"What exactly are you worried about?" He leaned forward, and the tiny hairs on her forearms stood up. "Are you afraid I'll make a move on you when I bring you home?"

"No."

Nervous or not, she was able to say that with complete confidence. She was one hundred percent certain that Rick Hunter would not be making a move on her tonight.

He sat back again, slowly. "All right, then, what? Are you always this uptight on dates?"

"Yes. I've never…I've never been any good at it."

He raised an eyebrow. "Did it ever occur to you that *they* weren't any good at it?"

"Who?" she asked, feeling confused.

"The men you went out with."

She blinked. "I'm pretty sure the problem is me. Why do you think it was them?"

"Because you didn't feel relaxed."

"I don't feel relaxed now," she reminded him. "So either you're no good, either, or it really is me."

He grinned at her. "I'm very, very good. And I'm just getting started. Twenty bucks says I have you relaxed in five minutes."

It was her turn to raise an eyebrow. "Five minutes, huh?" She could feel herself smiling again, a smile he'd drawn out of her. "Okay, give it your best shot."

"Tell me about the kids you work with."

That surprised her. "Really?"

"Yes. I'd like to know more about your foundation." He grinned at her again. "I just wrote you a pretty big check, in case you've forgotten. I have a vested interest in your organization."

Childhood cancer didn't really lend itself to casual conversation, which was why Allison avoided talking about her work on the rare occasions she went on a date. But Rick had asked her, and when she looked at him, all she could see in his green eyes was genuine interest.

"Okay."

She meant to stop after a story or two. But Rick was a surprisingly good listener, asking a few questions but mostly just absorbing what she said, and encouraging her with a nod here and there to keep talking.

They were interrupted twice, first by the sommelier to take their wine order and then by the waiter to take their dinner order. Their bottle of Burgundy arrived and the waiter filled their glasses deftly.

It was then that Allison realized she felt… relaxed.

"What do you know," she said, smiling across the table.

"What?"

"I guess I owe you twenty bucks. Has it been five minutes yet?"

A corner of his mouth lifted. "A little longer, I think."

"I'm still impressed."

He gestured toward her wineglass. "You'll be even more impressed when you taste that."

She reached for the glass to oblige him, raising it to her lips. She glanced at him over the rim, and their eyes met.

For a second she forgot what she was doing. Then she blinked, breaking the connection, and took a sip.

* * *

Rick had asked Allison about work because he knew it would put her at ease, and if he couldn't put her at ease his plan wouldn't succeed. No one would believe they were dating if Allison looked ready to jump out of her skin every time they were together.

She'd been so different at the hospital. Comfortable with him, comfortable with herself. He remembered the warmth he'd felt when she'd put her hand on his arm.

Of course the hospital was her domain, and she'd only touched him out of sympathy. Given the nature of her work, she probably did that a lot. Dating, on the other hand, wasn't something she did a lot.

But why?

She was passionate about her work. She was intelligent, dedicated, warm-hearted and generous.

And she was beautiful. The kind of beautiful

you wanted to stare at all night because it wasn't all on the surface. The more you looked, the more you saw—and the more you wanted to see.

So why was she still on the market? She'd said it was her choice, and considering she could have her pick of men, he believed her. She obviously wasn't a flirt. He'd given her openings—back at her apartment, and in the elevator, and a few minutes ago when he'd asked if she expected him to make a move on her tonight.

She hadn't taken the bait, and in spite of himself, he'd felt a twinge of disappointment. What would Allison look like flirting? What would she sound like? She was so straight-forward, so genuine and direct, it was hard to imagine her giving a sidelong glance or a sultry smile or using that low, sweet voice to make an innuendo.

Not that she needed to do any of that. She

was taking her first sip of the wine and he couldn't take his eyes off her. She set the glass back down on the table and smiled at him.

"Wow. I mean…*wow.*"

"I thought you'd like it," he said, feeling pleased. He was watching her taste it again when he noticed a familiar face a few tables away.

"Jackpot," he said, and Allison started to turn her head.

"No, don't look," he said quickly. "My God, this is perfect—even better than the *Gazette* reporter who just came in and sat down at the bar."

"What's perfect?" she whispered, leaning toward him.

He grinned at her. "My grandmother's best friend is here tonight, and she just got up from her table. I'm happy to report that we're between her and the restroom. We'll be seeing her in about ten seconds."

Rick managed to look surprised when the silver-haired woman paused at their table. "Shirley! I didn't know you were here tonight." He rose to his feet politely, giving the older woman a quick peck on the cheek. Allison had risen to her feet, as well.

"Mrs. Donovan, how nice to see you," she said.

Shirley looked startled. "It's nice to see you, too, Allison."

"Mrs. Donovan is one of the Star Foundation's patrons," Allison explained to Rick, who was obviously surprised that the women knew each other.

"For goodness' sakes, call me Shirley. I've known you for three years." Her sharp black eyes flickered between the two of them. "I must admit I'm a bit surprised to see the two of you together. Are you here on a—"

"Date? You bet," Rick said, smiling at Allison.

"Well, well. You'll pardon me, dear boy, if I say that I admire your taste more than Allison's. No offense, of course."

"None taken," Rick murmured. He knew Shirley's opinion of him was about on par with his grandmother's.

"Allison is a person whom I admire—and whom I've tried to fix up with my nephew several times. With no success, I might add. How did this good-looking rascal convince you to go out with him?"

Rick was about to answer for her, not wanting Allison to feel on the spot, but he never got the chance. "I lost a bet," Allison said cheerfully.

Shirley blinked. "A bet?"

"Rick said I couldn't beat him at darts after five shots of whiskey, and of course I had to take him on. My honor was at stake."

"Of course," Shirley said, starting to smile.

Rick was looking at Allison with his eyebrows raised.

"Alas, it turns out that Rick is some kind of darts prodigy. If his company ever folds, he could fall back on a career as a barroom hustler. His winnings were a date with me, and the rest is history."

"I see," Shirley said, shaking her head but still smiling. "I'll have to tell my nephew he's been using the wrong approach. Richard, I trust you'll treat this young lady well. She's not like your usual dinner companions."

"Believe me, I'm finding that out."

Rick watched her walk away, noting that she didn't make it five paces before she was pulling her cell phone out of her purse. Unless he missed his guess, his grandmother was about to get a call.

He turned back to Allison, who was grinning at him.

"I didn't realize you had such a gift for storytelling," he said as they sat down again.

"Well, now you know."

"On the bright side, I take it you still feel relaxed."

"I do. Relaxed enough to start asking *you* some questions."

He took a sip of wine. "What kind of questions?"

"The same thing you asked me. I'd like to know more about your work."

Their appetizers had arrived. Allison took a bite of her mushroom fritter, and he chased a piece of crab cake with another sip of Burgundy.

"What do you want to know?"

"How you got started, I guess. How you created a software empire."

"I wouldn't call Hunter Systems an empire. Do you really want to hear the whole story?"

"Of course I do. I wouldn't have asked if I wasn't interested."

That was the kind of thing people said on a first date, and most of the time it wasn't true. But when Allison said it, it never even occurred to him to doubt her.

They were finished with their appetizers by the time he went through the short version of his company's history—how he and an army buddy connected with a few friends from college and rented that first tiny office on Grand, only a few miles from where the company was now. How they'd worked round the clock, eating and even sleeping in the cramped space until they had a product ready to launch. How "Magician's Labyrinth" had hit big, making enough money to allow them to expand into other kinds of software.

"But you still make games?"

"Sure. Our gaming division puts out new products every year."

"But you don't? You personally, I mean."

He shook his head. "No time. And game design is a crazy job, best suited to kids. Kids at heart if not in years. And in case you hadn't noticed, I'm all grown up."

It was another not-so-subtle opportunity to flirt. She didn't take the bait, but at least this time she blushed.

The waiter brought their entrées, setting a dish of lobster ravioli in front of Allison and a steak with béarnaise sauce in front of him. He watched as she cut a ravioli in half and put it in her mouth, chewing and swallowing with a little *mmm* of pleasure that sent a bolt of awareness through him.

"Tell me why you don't date," he said abruptly.

He was breaking his cardinal rule with women—don't ask anything too personal, especially in the beginning. His relationships, such as they were, tended to skim across the surface.

But he wasn't actually dating Allison, and he really wanted to know the answer.

Allison looked down at her plate, swirling the other half of her ravioli in cream sauce. "That's not important," she said.

"It is to me. I'd like to know."

She looked up at him, her blue eyes guarded. "It's not exactly my favorite topic. My family brings it up all the time, and it makes me crazy. Especially when I think there are so many more important things going on in the world than whether or not I go out on dates."

"Like what?" he asked, taking a bite of his steak but keeping his eyes on hers.

"Like everything. Disease, poverty, natural disasters. And that's just off the top of my head."

He poured a little more Burgundy into her

glass. "Okay, you've got me there. But I'm still curious."

She frowned down at her wineglass, tracing the rim with a fingertip. "There's not a lot to say. I was pretty serious about someone in high school, but then we broke up, and it just… turned me off the whole scene. I've gone out with people here and there, but I haven't been in a relationship since. And at some point I realized I didn't miss it."

She looked up at him. "My work and my family are the most important things in my life. I don't need a relationship to feel complete. And I think romance can be a distraction, you know? Because emotions are overwhelming, and it's easy to give in to them. Because it feels good for a while. And when it stops feeling good, the pain becomes an excuse, too. I don't want to get out of bed because so-and-so left me. I can't go to work today because I saw him out with another girl, boo-hoo, boo-hoo.

And meanwhile, there are people out there with real problems, really hurting. And—" She paused suddenly and took a breath. "And anyway, that's why I don't date."

He'd forgotten to eat, watching and listening to her. If he'd hoped that getting an answer to his question would take the edge off his curiosity, that hope was now shot to hell.

"So love is just an escape?"

She lifted her chin slightly, as if sensing a challenge. "I think it can be an illusion. And I think people can indulge in it like a drug, because it's just as addictive and distracting."

"So people in love are just deluding themselves? What about married couples?"

She bit her lip. "See? That's why I don't talk about this. I know I come off sounding like I'm looking down on people or something, and I don't mean to. Of course I don't think all married people are deluding themselves. My parents have a good marriage. But it's not *romantic*. They work too hard for that. They're farmers, and they've worked hard all their lives. I know they love each other, but they're not indulgent about it. They don't make a fuss."

"So it's okay to be in love if you don't make a fuss?"

She sighed. "Let's just forget it, okay? I'm sorry I ever answered your question."

"I'm not."

"I suppose you think you have some kind of insight into me now."

"I don't know about that. But it's obvious you've been on some lousy dates—and that whatever happened with your high school boyfriend hit you pretty hard."

She frowned. "The way I feel about romance isn't because of one experience."

"But he was a factor, wasn't he?"

"I think he was just a catalyst."

"A catalyst for what?"

"For deciding that I wanted to put my energies into something more meaningful."

"Unlike love."

"Unlike romantic love, yes. But there's plenty of love in my life. My family, my friends… and my work is all about love. I love the kids I work with. I care about their families. If I didn't, I wouldn't do what I do."

Rick drained his glass and refilled it, topping off Allison's afterward. "So it's only romance you don't believe in."

"I'm willing to believe romantic love exists. I'm just not interested in it, at least at this point in my life. And what about you?" she countered. "That night at the coffee shop, I got the impression you're less interested in romance than I am. Are you telling me I was wrong? That you do believe in love?"

He was glad she asked. It was good to be reminded of the fact that he didn't believe in much of anything, before he let himself get too drawn in by Allison's beguiling eyes and her warm heart and most of all her fascinating prickly side, the side that said *I won't, I won't*…and made a man want to persuade her to say *I will.*

He shrugged. "My parents had a rotten marriage, which made it hard to believe in romance. And I let go of the illusion completely in my twenties, when I found out the girl I'd fallen for was a con artist in training. The only difference now is that I actually seek out mercenary women. That way there aren't any unpleasant surprises, and I never feel guilty about ending things."

She stared at him, her hand frozen on her wineglass. "You're really that cynical?"

"Yes."

"You can't honestly believe a woman would only be with you because of money."

He raised an eyebrow. "Tell me again why you're here tonight?"

That made her blush, but she didn't back down. "This deal was your idea, not mine—and I'm not interested in dating anyone, so you know it's not personal. But even though I'm not exactly a cheerleader for romance, I know there are lots of women out there who would fall for you even if you didn't have a dime."

Which was the last thing he wanted.

He shook his head. "I'm not interested in a serious relationship. I guess I'm like you—more interested in work. Even though I'm not as passionate about my work as you are."

She rested her chin in her hand as she looked at him, the candlelight making her skin glow. "You're not?"

"Well…not lately."

"But you were passionate when you designed 'Magician's Labyrinth.'"

He remembered the long, feverish nights at his computer. "Yeah, I was. But that was a long time ago."

"My sister says that when you love your work, you'll do it till you bleed. And that's how you'll know you're in the right job."

He thought back again to his design days, to sleepless nights and blurred vision and the gnawing in his stomach when he realized he'd forgotten to eat. "What does your sister do?"

"Jenna's a musician. I found her practicing guitar one day when she was thirteen or fourteen, and her fingers really were bleeding. She'd only had the guitar a week and her hands weren't callused yet. That's the day she told me she knew what she wanted to do with her life."

She leaned forward. "When's the last time you designed something?"

That made him think of Carol, and his VP of product development. The two of them were always bugging him to get back to the creative side of software, rather than sticking to the business side.

"It's been a while," he said.

She was studying him, her eyes much too intelligent, and he wished he hadn't been so persistent in asking her questions. It made turnabout seem like fair play.

"How old were you when you first thought of 'Magician's Labyrinth'? When the idea first came to you?"

"It was my freshman year in college, so I guess I was eighteen or nineteen."

"How old were you when your mother died?"

His jaw tightened. "I was seventeen."

"So it was pretty soon afterward you started working on the game."

His face felt stiff. "And that's significant because?"

"I'm just thinking about that character, the one Julie was playing. He got killed, remember? But you saved him. There was that healing spell woven into his armor. The spell that brought him back from death."

The stiffness spread into his muscles, hardening his spine. "So?"

"I think the game was your way of dealing with all the emotions you felt after losing your mother. You created something that came out of real feeling, out of the love you had for her and the pain you felt when she died. That's why the game connects with people, why people like Julie love it so much. Because it came out of something genuine. If you could connect with that part of yourself again, with your imagination and creativity, I think you could make something new. Something even more wonderful."

Rick knew Allison wasn't probing his soft spots because he'd probed hers. But the fact was, he'd pushed her to talk to him when he wasn't willing to talk to her. Not about this kind of thing.

"Let's change the subject."

She looked at him for a moment, and

something about her eyes made him feel like it didn't matter if he talked about himself or not—that she could still see inside him, some-how.

It wasn't a comfortable feeling.

"Of course," she said after a moment. "I'm sorry I got so personal. I think it must be the wine…I don't usually drink so much." She finished the last bite of her ravioli and pushed her plate away, propping her chin on her hand again. "What do you usually talk about on a first date?"

He drank the last of his Burgundy and set the empty glass back on the table. "Nothing too earth-shaking. Music, movies, sports. Current events if they're not too political."

She smiled at him. "Well, you know I like movies. Let's give that a try."

The waiter came by with the dessert menu.

Though not as charged as their earlier conversation, it turned out that talking with

Allison about movies was just as stimulating. It wasn't the topic—it was her. She was fun to talk to.

And to look at.

He watched as Allison savored the last bite of her molten chocolate cake and set her spoon down beside her dish. Not satisfied, she used her index finger to capture the last streaks of chocolate from the inside of the bowl and popped her finger in her mouth, licking the chocolate off with obvious enjoyment.

His body tightened and he struggled to tamp down the sudden flash of desire. He knew Allison had absolutely no idea how sexy she looked doing that and she'd be shocked if he told her.

But he was starting to think this dating deal was going to be harder on him than it was on her.

The ride back to her apartment was quiet. He looked over at Allison as he pulled up in front of her apartment building, and saw that she'd fallen asleep.

He turned off the engine, thinking that might wake her, but her eyes stayed closed and in the sudden silence he could hear her soft, even breathing.

His left arm rested on the steering wheel as he watched her. Her lips were parted and looked impossibly soft. Her chest rose and fell with each breath, and even her heavy suit jacket couldn't entirely hide the curve of her breasts beneath.

"Allison," he said softly, then reached over and shook her gently. "Allison."

Opening her eyes, she blinked at him. "Did I fall asleep?" She sat upright and scrubbed her face with her hands. "Wow, that's embarrassing. I bet none of your real dates ever did that."

She glanced out the window. "Oh, we're

here." She opened her door and got out of the car before he could say anything.

"Sorry," she said, looking up at him when he joined her on the sidewalk. "I should have waited for you to come around and open the door, right? Isn't that the proper dating etiquette?"

"As you keep reminding me, this wasn't a real date." He hesitated a moment. "Did you have a good time?"

"I did, actually," she said, sounding almost surprised. She leaned back against the car, her hands in the pockets of her jacket, and he leaned back, too. "It wasn't boring," she added, and that made him smile.

They stayed like that for a couple of minutes, their shoulders almost touching, looking at Allison's apartment building and the three quarter moon that hung above it.

If this were a real date, he'd make his move right now. He'd step in front of her, and press her back against the car so she could feel him against her, chest to knees. Then he'd slide his hands into her hair and capture that soft, sweet mouth with his…

Of course this wasn't a real date. But almost without realizing it, he moved just a little closer to her, until his shoulder brushed against hers.

She pushed herself away from the car like a shot, turning back to face him after she was a few feet away.

"Good night, Rick. And thanks for dinner."

He held himself still. "Good night, Allison. I'll call you this week to set up our next date, okay?"

"Sure." She gave him a quick smile and then hurried toward the door of her building. She fumbled with her key for a few seconds, turned to wave, and then disappeared inside.

After a minute, he saw the lights in her apartment go on.

After another minute, he realized he was still

standing there, picturing Allison finally taking off that heavy jacket as she got ready for bed.

He shook his head slowly.

One date into their bargain, and he was wishing he was up there with her. He wondered what kind of shape he'd be in after three months.

And if she'd ever look at him the way he wanted her to.

Chapter Five

At seven the next morning, Allison's phone rang.

She reached for it without opening her eyes. "Hello?"

"Allison, is that you? Do you realize you're in the *newspaper?* Apparently you were on a date last night with Richard Hunter. The CEO of Hunter Systems. The man featured in *People* magazine as the Playboy of the Midwest. I tell you all this because it obviously slipped your mind. Otherwise, I'm sure you would have mentioned it to your family."

Allison sat up in bed, now fully awake. "Good morning to you, too, Mom."

Irene Landry sighed. "I just don't understand it. You're such a wonderful girl, so smart, so caring, so beautiful. Every night I lie awake, thinking that you're going to die alone, surrounded by cats—"

"Dying alone is not possible when you're a Landry, my building doesn't allow cats, and you go to bed every night at nine-thirty and sleep like a log, so I find it hard to picture you lying awake thinking about anything, much less your perfectly happy single daughter who—"

"Who, apparently, is no longer single!"

"Mom! Would you calm down for a second, please?"

"Oh, for goodness' sakes. I'm calm. Just tell me about this young man of yours. It'll be good practice for you, because as soon as the rest of the family wakes up and sees the paper, your phone will be ringing off the hook."

Allison groaned. "Which paper?"

"The *Gazette.* It's in the local news section."

"Local news? That's ridiculous. The most a story like this should rate is the gossip column. What's journalism coming to?"

"I guess it was a slow news day. Anyway, it's in there. Three photos—you look very pretty in all of them, although it looks like you're wearing a business suit. The headline...wait a second, let me get it...oh, yes. 'Has The Playboy of the Midwest Finally Found Love?' I must say, they wrote some very complimentary things about you and the Star Foundation."

"You know, Rick warned me this would happen, and I meant to call you yesterday, but I—" spent an hour standing in front of her closet, only to pick out a business suit. "I guess I forgot."

"Apparently. Well, fill me in now, before I explode."

She hadn't really thought through exactly what she'd tell her family. The whole truth? Well…maybe not. Not at seven in the morning on a Sunday, when she hadn't even had her coffee.

"The newspaper blew things way out of proportion. Rick and I met because of a patient I'm working with, and because he's made a big donation to the Star Foundation. We went to dinner last night as friends. No romance, Mom. Rick did warn me there might be a newspaper story or two, but—"

"Don't be silly."

"What?"

"Allison, go get the paper. Look at the pictures. Then try telling me that you and Richard Hunter are just friends."

She blinked. "Huh?"

"Just do it. Go get your paper and call me back."

What could she be talking about, Allison wondered as she put on her pink bunny slippers and plaid robe.

The doorbell rang before she was halfway across the living room.

She opened the door to find the *Gazette* lying on the mat, and Mrs. Kiersted from the apartment next door peering at her nearsightedly. "You're in the paper. Did you know? You look pretty good, too. Even though you're dressed like an undercover policewoman. Next time, put on a skirt. Is he in there with you? If he hasn't woken up yet, you should take a shower before he sees you. Your hair's sticking up all over the place."

Allison blushed and grabbed the paper from the mat. "Shame on you, Mrs. Kiersted.

When have I ever had a man in my apartment overnight?"

"Never, sweet pea. I guess even a blind squirrel finds an acorn once in a while, eh?"

"Goodbye, Mrs. Kiersted," Allison said with what she hoped was frosty dignity. Then she shut her door and retreated back into her apartment.

She decided caffeine would be required to cope with this situation, so she carried the paper into the kitchen and dropped it on the breakfast table before turning on the coffeemaker. Forcing herself to focus on the task at hand, she drummed her fingers on the counter as the hot fragrant liquid filled her red mug, adding cream and plenty of sugar before finally sitting down at the table, taking a sustaining sip and opening the paper to the local news section.

Three photos of them at dinner, just like her mother had said.

In the first one, she was talking with her hands as she leaned forward across the table. Rick was smiling as he listened to her, his eyes on her face.

In the second picture Rick was laughing, his eyes crinkled up, and she was resting her chin in her hand as she looked at him, a smile tugging at the corners of her mouth.

In the last picture their expressions were more serious, almost intense. Rick was talking in this one, his wineglass in his hand as he leaned toward her. She was leaning forward too, her posture dynamic, and the energy between them seemed…charged.

All three had one thing in common. The man and woman captured in these photos seemed completely absorbed in one another, as if nothing else existed.

Allison sat back in her chair and frowned. Then she called her mother.

"Okay, I see how you could get the wrong

idea from those pictures. But that's just be-cause we were interested in what we were talking about. I probably look like that when I'm talking to my female friends, too."

"Allison, the attraction between you and that man practically zings off the page."

"Sorry, mom. If anything was zinging it was our conversation. And in that last pic-ture I think we were arguing about something. That's not romantic."

"Are you kidding? Your father and I argued all the time when we were dating. I think that's why he fell in love with me. I was the only person who ever stood up to him."

Her parents seemed so comfortable together it was hard to imagine them ever dating, ever falling in love, ever anything but married. Al-lison put that disconcerting image aside and focused on the issue at hand. "Mom, I think I would know if I was in a romantic relation-ship with Rick Hunter. And I'm definitely not.

In fact, we made a point of telling each other we're not physically attracted to each other. So there wouldn't be any misunderstandings."

"You made a point of that, did you?"

"Yes."

Irene's snort was clearly audible. "I'm going to make a wager about this, and you know my track record." Her mother was famous in the Landry clan for having never once lost a bet.

Allison felt a wave of unease. "Look, Mom, no betting. Okay? Don't even finish that thought. I'll see you in two weeks for Jenna and Jake's birthday. In the meantime, please try to accept the fact that Rick and I are just friends."

It was a few more minutes before she managed to actually say goodbye, but Allison barely had time to breathe a sigh of relief before the phone rang again. This time it was her aunt Beth, wanting the scoop on her niece's exciting new boyfriend.

A few hours later, she was sitting in the living room with a book and her third cup of coffee when the phone rang for what had to be the seventeenth time. She grabbed it and hit the talk button.

"What," she growled.

"Wow. Not a morning person, huh?"

Rick.

A rush of sensation shot through her. She almost dropped the phone.

"Sorry," she said. "I thought you were another member of the Landry family, calling to give me the third degree."

"They saw the paper?"

"A big yes to that."

"What did you end up telling them?"

"I just said we were friends and that the *Gazette* blew things out of proportion."

"Did they buy it?"

"Of course," Allison said. "I mean, why wouldn't they?" Her eye fell on the newspaper she'd set down on the coffee table, and she wondered what Rick had thought when he first saw the pictures.

"No reason. I'm just wondering how rough your morning was."

"I'd call it medium rough. The phone's been ringing off the hook but at least they all believe me."

"Well, that's good. My grandmother also saw the paper, by the way. And she heard from Shirley Donovan last night."

She'd forgotten for a moment what last night had been about. "And?"

"And we're invited to afternoon tea at Hunter Hall."

"Afternoon tea? I didn't know people actually did that. Not in the New World, anyway. When does she want us to come?"

"Next Sunday at three o'clock, if that works for you."

In spite of herself, her stomach fluttered at

the thought of seeing him again. "Um, yes. Yes, that's fine."

"I just hope your family doesn't harass you too much between now and then."

Allison sighed. "You know what they say when I beg them to leave me alone? They tell me that being pestered is just one of the consequences of being loved. How's that for an excuse to invade someone's privacy?"

He laughed, and Allison caught herself smiling at the phone.

"That sounds like something my grandmother would say." They chatted for a few more minutes before saying goodbye. When he hung up, Allison sat listening to the dial tone for a moment. Then she turned the phone off and set it back down on the coffee table.

The only thing between them was a business deal.

So it didn't make sense that she already missed the sound of his voice.

* * *

Unless she was right in front of him, Rick didn't usually think too much about whatever woman he happened to be dating. Of course, he wasn't actually *dating* Allison, as he reminded himself every time she popped up in his thoughts that week.

But while his mind understood there was nothing between them but business, his body hadn't gotten the memo.

The Sunday *Gazette* was still on his kitchen counter, folded to page thirty-six. Every so often he'd glance at the pictures, comparing them to his memory of Allison that night. They didn't do justice to her beauty, but they did capture a little of her energy. Even in black and white you could see how alive she was, how intense.

He remembered her sweetness, too. The openhearted generosity that had been so apparent when she talked about the families she worked with. And he remembered the way she challenged him about his own work, suggesting he go back to the creative side of his job.

He couldn't help imagining what it would be like to have her sweetness—and her fire—in his bed. A part of him—a very primitive part—wanted to be the man who could change her mind about staying single, who could make her want him as much as he wanted her.

Of course he'd never act on that desire. After all, it was her lack of interest that made her so perfect for his plan. Even if he could change her mind—which seemed highly unlikely—the last thing he needed was to get tangled up with a woman like Allison, a woman who deserved so much more than he could ever offer.

But knowing that didn't stop him from thinking about her.

The piece in the *Gazette* drew a comment or two at work. Carol let him know she wanted details at some point, and it turned out that his VP of product development, a software engineer named Derek Brown, had known Allison for a few years.

"I met her when my nephew was diagnosed with leukemia. There was a bad time when we weren't sure he was going to make it, and the Star Foundation arranged to have someone bring in all my sister's meals, clean her house and do a lot of the other stuff she couldn't focus on. And Allison was with us in the hospital every chance she got. Jimmy's crazy about her. He's in remission now, but they still email each other once in a while. I'm telling you, man, Allison is something else. I hope you appreciate how lucky you are."

Rick added the Star Foundation's website to his internet favorites. Every so often he clicked on the link and read a little about Allison or her company, and looked at the one picture of Allison posted there.

And one day after work he went to a book-store and picked up her memoir, the one she'd published in college.

It sat on his nightstand for three days, untouched. He'd always avoided reading anything about cancer, although several well-meaning friends, neighbors and relatives had given him a variety of books to choose from after his mother's death.

This was different, of course. He was eighteen years older, and he was interested in this book because of Allison, not because of the subject. Still, it wasn't until Saturday night that he finally opened it.

He'd gone to see Julie that afternoon, a visit highlighted by the joyful news that she was doing well and would be going home soon. Her parents had been there, along with her sister and two brothers, and the day had felt like a celebration.

After a quiet night at home with Chinese

takeout and ESPN, he went to bed around eleven, but found he was too restless to sleep. He debated turning on the TV, hesitated a moment, and then picked up Allison's book from his nightstand. He looked at the back cover first, at the younger version of Allison smiling out at him. Then he turned to page one and started to read.

Once again Allison was standing in front of her closet, but this time she had Rachel with her. Rachel knew the whole story of the deal with Rick—Allison had broken down and told her the truth after swearing her to secrecy. It shouldn't have mattered to her what Allison wore today, but her friend was shaking her head back and forth with a pained expression on her face.

"This is just…wow. I've probably seen every outfit you own at one point or another, but to see them all together like this...wow. This is one depressing wardrobe."

"Thank you. That's very encouraging."

"I wasn't trying to encourage you. This is more in the nature of an intervention."

"I just need something to wear to afternoon tea. How hard can that be?"

Rachel sighed. "Do we have time to go shopping?"

"He'll be here in half an hour."

"I wish I'd known about this date before I came for brunch. I could have picked something up on my way over."

"It's not a date. And I don't want to buy anything new for a nondate. I don't want to go out of my way, you know? That would make it seem too..."

"Real?"

"Well, yes."

"I know it's not a real date—technically, anyway. But you're going out with a guy you like, and if you tell me you don't care how you look I just won't believe you."

"I don't *like* like him."

"My God, how old are you? And you know that line in Shakespeare about protesting too much? I'm thinking it applies here. Look me in the eyes, Allison Landry, and tell me you don't give a single damn what Rick Hunter thinks of you. And I don't just mean your mind or your heart or your bright shiny soul. You care what he thinks when he looks at you, too."

Allison opened her mouth to deny it, but the words stuck in her throat. She felt her face turning red, as if she'd just admitted something shameful. She slumped down on the edge of her bed, and Rachel sat down next to her.

"Don't look so tragic," her friend said gently. "This isn't a bad thing. It's a good thing."

Allison shook her head slowly. "How can you say this is a good thing? I have a crush on Rick Hunter! Just saying it out loud sounds ridiculous. You saw that article in *People*—you know the kind of women he typically goes out with. He's only spending time with me because I'm a means to an end. And because he thinks I'm not attracted to him."

She wrapped her arms around her stomach. "Why *am* I attracted to him? It doesn't really make sense. He's so different from me, so—"

"Are you kidding? Maybe you're attracted to him because you're not blind."

"You think I'm that superficial?"

"I think you're that human. And maybe you like him *because* he's different from you. Because he challenges you. And you haven't been on a date in more than a year. What's wrong with cutting loose a little?"

"Nothing, I guess. It's just…I don't want to make a fool of myself."

"You won't." Rachel smiled as she reminisced. "Back in college, I had a huge crush on one of my professors. He was twenty years older and happily married, and I never even thought about acting on it, but boy, did I love going to that class. Why don't you just let yourself enjoy what you're feeling? Rick never has to know. Sometimes feeling attracted to someone can be an end in itself."

An end in itself. That was a new idea, something that had never even occurred to her.

Rachel got up from the bed and went over to the closet, where she pulled out a pair of khaki pants and a blue cotton sweater.

"Here," she said. "The pants are boring but the sweater is exactly the color of your eyes. And it's lightweight enough for the warm weather."

Glad to have the decision taken out of her hands, Allison put the outfit on. Then she and Rachel studied her reflection in the mirror that hung on the closet door.

"It'll do," Rachel said after a moment. "I

know I won't be able to talk you into full makeup, but how about a touch of something? A dab of concealer under your eyes, maybe some lipstick?"

"I suppose I—"

"Great," Rachel said briskly, grabbing a couple of tubes from her purse. She told Allison to look up as she applied the concealer with practiced ease, and then let her friend put on the lip gloss herself. It was a soft rose shade and wasn't obvious, Allison noted with relief when she looked at herself in the mirror. Just a little extra shine, a little extra color.

"You look great," Rachel assured her, and Allison smiled at her in the mirror. "Thanks," she said.

"No problem. And now I should be heading home."

"I'll walk you out."

The spring day was so gorgeous that Allison decided to wait outside for Rick. He arrived at three o'clock exactly, and despite her best efforts to remain unfazed, she couldn't control the sudden pounding of her heart or the smile that spread across her face when he got out of his sleek black car.

He was smiling, too, but his eyes were hidden behind a pair of sunglasses that probably cost more than her secondhand truck. They exchanged hellos as he came up to her.

"How was your week?" he asked.

"Busy, but good. How was yours?"

"The same."

He took off his glasses, tucking them in a pocket. Allison felt a little inward shiver when his green eyes met hers.

He took a step closer, his eyes tracing over her face.

"You're wearing lip gloss," he said suddenly.

She cursed Rachel silently. "Um, yes." His gaze was directed at her mouth, and she licked her lips nervously. "It's flavored," she blurted out, realizing it for the first time as she tasted strawberries.

His gaze traveled up her face to her eyes. "What?"

"I—" She'd completely lost her place in the conversation and could only stare back at him, at the intense green eyes under dark brows and tousled hair, at the almost imperceptible twitching of a muscle at the corner of his jaw, and at his mobile, sensitive mouth.

He swallowed, then took a step back to open the passenger door for her. "Ready to go?"

"Sure," she said quickly, avoiding his eyes as she stepped into the car, settling into the soft leather seat and buckling her safety belt with shaking hands.

What the heck was that? It had almost seemed like he was going to kiss her, or wanted to kiss her, or something. And she'd practically asked him to. *It's flavored*, she'd said—a moment destined to become one of those that stick with you for all time, never losing its ability to make you squirm with embarrassment.

Rick slid into the driver's seat and turned the key in the ignition. "Any music preferences for the ride?"

She loved music, but at the moment she couldn't think of a single artist or album or genre. "What's in your CD player right now?"

He hit the play button, and Louis Armstrong and Ella Fitzgerald started singing a duet. "How's this?" he asked, pulling away from the curb.

"Perfect," she said, surprised. She wouldn't have figured him for an Ella Fitzgerald fan.

He smiled at her, and her tension started to ease away. "Okay, I know you like the classics. Big band music and old movies. What about the modern era? What have you seen this year that you liked?"

As they talked, she let herself look at him, a

move made easy since Rick kept his eyes on the road most of the time.

He was wearing a short-sleeved white polo shirt, and she found her gaze lingering on his arms. The exact point his deltoids gave way to the swell of his biceps and triceps...the play of hard muscle beneath smooth skin...the flex and release of his forearms as he drove.

She noticed other things, too. The fine lines at the corners of his eyes when he laughed. The faint scent of his aftershave. The warm, deep voice that seemed to vibrate somewhere in her chest.

There was a kind of doubling in her awareness. She was interested in their conversation, entertained by Rick's agile intelligence and original mind. But she was conscious of him physically, too. Her nerves tingled. Every inch of her skin felt sensitized. And the left side of her body, the side nearest to him, felt warm, as if he were radiating heat.

The drive gave her time to get used to the awareness. As she and Rick continued to talk, she felt more confident that she could hide it. Not that she could submerge it completely, but that she could keep it at bay—enough, at least, to keep from blushing like a teenager every time their eyes met.

Maybe Rachel had been right. Maybe she could enjoy this feeling, as long as she kept it buried deep, where it belonged.

Their discussion veered toward politics. At one point Allison was arguing so fiercely against a position Rick had defended that it took her a few minutes to notice a suspicious twitch at the corner of his mouth.

"What's so funny?" she asked.

"Nothing. I agree with you, that's all."

"What? Then why did you say—"

"I like hearing you argue," he said. "I like how committed you are. When you're all riled up like that I feel like I can see right into you."

Exactly what she wanted to avoid. "What do you mean?"

She saw him reaching for words, his dark brows drawing a little closer together. "When you talk about something you care about, you don't hide who you are. You just put yourself out there. You don't give a damn what anyone else might think."

When it came to things like politics, maybe he was right. But she didn't want more credit for honesty than she deserved. "There are plenty of things I keep to myself."

"I'm sure there are. But the things you do tell me are honest, and that's what I like. Most of the women I go out with are so busy trying to figure out what I think, and then agreeing with me, that I never have a clue what they actually believe in—if anything."

She stared at him. "Why would anyone do that? Hide their real opinions that way?"

He shrugged. "Believe it or not, there are

actually women out there who only want to marry a millionaire. And they'll do whatever they can to make that happen." There was a tinge of bitterness in his voice, and Allison felt an unexpected rush of anger.

"That's disgusting. Women shouldn't go out with you because you're rich. They should go out with you because you're—" She paused.

He looked at her. "Because I'm what?"

"Because you're nice." Her cheeks felt hot.

He waited a moment. "Just nice?" he finally prodded, one eyebrow raised.

She rolled her eyes. "I can't believe you're fishing for compliments. And, anyway, you just told me how honest and forthright I am. Don't expect any help from me in the ego-stroking department."

"Honest and annoying. Did I mention annoying?"

"Nope, you left that one out."

They'd left the highway several minutes

ago, and now they turned into a long, curving driveway that ran through a belt of oak trees. Allison sat up straighter in her seat, curious for her first glimpse of Hunter Hall. When it came into view as they emerged from the woods, she took a deep breath.

"Oh, Rick. It's beautiful."

And it was. The ivy-covered stone blended into the landscape of old growth trees, spring flowers made a splash of color here and there, and she could tell that in the full flush of summer the surrounding gardens would be absolutely glorious.

She could understand why Rick loved this place so much. The neo-Gothic architecture appealed to the imagination, and the man who'd designed "Magician's Labyrinth" had imagination to spare.

As he came around to open her door—she waited for him this time—she pictured the house and gardens filled with kids and their families. This was the kind of place she wanted for her center. A place to spark the imagination, a place full of beauty.

"You really like it?" Rick asked her as she got out of the car and stood beside him. The two of them stood looking up at the house for a moment, at the turrets and gables and the windows that sparkled like diamonds in the bright sunlight.

"Are you kidding? Of course I do. This place is definitely worth bribing a woman to be your fake girlfriend."

He nudged her with his elbow, catching her in a ticklish spot, and she giggled. "It wasn't a bribe, it was a negotiation."

"If you say so. Which reminds me…do we need to get our stories straight, or anything like that? Before we meet your grandmother."

"Not unless you're going to exercise your talent for fiction like you did with Shirley."

She smiled. "Nope, no tall tales today. Actually, I don't see any reason why we can't stick pretty close to the truth. We met because of Julie's wish, and because you made a big donation to the Star Foundation. After we visited Julie in the hospital, you asked me out. End of story."

"Makes sense," Rick agreed.

They were quiet for a moment, looking at the house. Allison turned to ask Rick when it had been built, but the question stuck in her throat when she saw him looking at her.

"Ready to go in?"

She nodded. He held out his arm the way he had in her apartment, and she only hesitated a moment before she slid her hand into the crook of his arm.

This time, though, he was wearing short sleeves, and her fingers tingled where they touched his warm bare skin. And as they walked side by side up the stone walkway toward the house, she prayed he couldn't hear the sudden pounding of her heart.

Chapter Six

The heavy front door opened just as they reached it. And there was Gran, elegant in a Chanel suit and a cloud of expensive perfume, a welcoming smile on her face.

Rick couldn't remember the last time he'd seen his grandmother at the door like this. Meredith, her longtime housekeeper, usually met visitors and let them into Hunter Hall.

It was because of Allison, he realized with a twinge of guilt. Gran was excited to meet her.

"My dears, how wonderful to see you!" She

gave Rick a brief smile and turned immediately to Allison. "You're as lovely as your picture in the paper," she said, giving her a quick peck on each cheek. "Now come inside, you two. We'll have our tea in the south parlor, but I thought Allison might like to see Hunter Hall first."

"I'd love that," Allison said, and Gran smiled at her again before ushering them inside and launching into the tour Rick had heard her give a hundred times before.

He fell in behind the two women as they went through the house, through the nine bedrooms, the upstairs and downstairs parlors, the game room and music room, the library and gallery, the conservatory, the dining room, the ballroom—and he let the old, familiar magic of Hunter Hall settle over him as his thoughts wandered, and as he watched Allison talking and laughing with his grandmother, who insisted she call her Evie.

They made an unlikely pair. His grand-mother was such a…finished product, her suit accessorized with jewelry and a Hermès scarf, her white hair exquisitely styled, her high heels clicking busily on the marble floor of the upstairs gallery.

And then there was Allison, slim and grace-ful, a diamond in the rough with her khaki pants and blue cotton sweater and scuffed bal-lerina flats, no jewelry, no accessories, and the short, no-nonsense haircut that left her neck enticingly bare.

They paused in front of a painting by John Singer Sargent, a portrait of his great-great-grandmother that had been commissioned after her marriage to Cyrus Hunter. Gran was talking about the family connection to the artist while Allison studied the painting with her hands in her pockets, nodding every so often as she listened.

He was standing behind them, but he wasn't

listening to the lecture and he wasn't looking at the portrait. His eyes were on Allison, on the nape of her neck, and he drifted closer without realizing it, breathing in her fresh, sweet fragrance, like soap and shampoo and sunlight.

Close enough to touch her.

He wished he had the right to do that. He longed to run the tips of his fingers lightly over her bare skin, to feel her shiver in response.

He took a deep breath and tried to get a grip on himself.

I want her.

It had been building up all week, a week of not seeing her but thinking about her, looking at those pictures in the *Gazette* and reading her book, full of love and grief and anger and hope and all the raw, naked emotions he'd packed away so long ago.

And then he got to her apartment and saw

the shimmer of lip gloss on that perfect mouth, and thought for a second that she felt attracted to him, and had highlighted those already tempting lips in a feminine effort to appeal to a man. To appeal to *him*. And in that same instant, he'd realized how much he wanted it to be true.

Because he wanted her. He wanted her with an intensity that had almost overwhelmed him as he stood there on the sidewalk, staring at that sweet, soft, tantalizing mouth, wanting to kiss her so badly his own mouth had gone dry. Then she'd said something, he wasn't sure what, and when he'd met her eyes she'd looked like a deer in the headlights, terrified he was going to act on the desire she must have read in his face.

He knew what an invitation to a kiss looked like, and it sure as hell wasn't that. And so he'd controlled himself, and pulled back, and her obvious relief was further proof she didn't feel the same way. That however much he might want to believe it, she hadn't put on lip gloss today because of him.

And that was okay, he told himself. If he was desperate for a kiss there were plenty of women out there who'd give him one. He and Allison had a business arrangement with clear boundaries and a clear goal. And unlike a relationship, Hunter Hall could be counted on to last forever.

He was telling himself all these things as he stared at her, his hands itching with the need to touch her, when his grandmother must have finished her lecture on Sargent. Allison took a step back and bumped right into him, and he put his hands on her shoulders without thinking, to steady her.

"Sorry," she apologized, twisting her head around to look up at him. "I didn't realize you were there."

"No problem," he said, his voice sounding

a little harsh in his own ears. He cleared his throat, but instead of releasing her, his hands tightened.

"Well," his grandmother said, "that concludes our tour." She was beaming at them, and Allison probably noticed, because instead of jerking out of his grasp she pulled away gently.

Lesson learned, he thought, his hands still tingling from the brief contact. He'd better not touch her like that again, because there was a good chance he might not let go.

Now his grandmother led the two of them down the main staircase and into the sun-drenched south parlor.

"I brought out some old photo albums I thought you might enjoy," she said to Allison, waving her over to the cream-colored sofa by the French windows. Allison went, and Rick followed, shooting daggers at his grandmother when she met his eyes.

"Don't give me that look," she said. "There's no harm in letting Allison see what a cute little boy you were. You can look through these while I tell Meredith we're ready for tea."

She went briskly out of the room again as Allison sat down. Rick sighed in resignation and sat down beside her, noticing how the late afternoon sunlight picked out the gold strands in her hair.

"I can't believe she dragged those out," he muttered as Allison lifted up one of the albums from the coffee table.

Allison grinned at him. "She doesn't do this every time you bring a woman over?"

"I try to avoid bringing women here. And when I do, my grandmother doesn't like them. That's how we ended up in this situation, remember?"

"Hmm. So, are you going to look at these pictures with me?"

"Absolutely not."

"Coward," she said, her blue eyes laughing at him.

"Have I mentioned lately how annoying you are?"

"Yes," she said, settling back against the armrest and opening the album. She held it so he couldn't see what she was looking at. "Oh, that's *adorable*," she said, the corners of her mouth twitching. "That's the cutest expression I've ever seen on a naked three-year-old."

He tried to swipe the book away from her, but she snatched it out of his reach.

"Ooh, here's one in the bathtub. Your butt is even cuter in this one."

"So help me, Allison—"

She grinned at him over the top of the album. "Why don't you look at them with me? I promise we'll skip right over the naked ones."

"No."

"Oh, come on. It'll be fun."

When her eyes glinted with mischief like

that, she was just about irresistible. "Fine. I'll do it if you'll reciprocate."

"Reciprocate? How could I do that?"

"By letting me see your childhood pictures. Preferably at your family home, with at least one relative telling me what an adorable little girl you were."

"You're actually volunteering to meet my family?"

"As long as I get to look at your photo albums."

She shook her head at him. "There aren't any albums of just me. You'll have to sit through pages and pages of group shots, and pictures of Megan, my brother Jake and my sister Jenna, not to mention aunts and uncles and cousins. You'll beg me to let you off after five minutes."

He grinned. "Twenty bucks says I last longer than you do."

"It's a bet," she said, scooting over next to

him. They weren't quite touching, but she laid the photo album down so one side rested on her leg and one side on his.

He was distracted by how close she was until he saw the pictures. "I hoped you were kidding about the bathtub shot. Grandmothers have no shame."

"Did she take all these?"

"Most of them. I came to visit a few times a year, and my grandmother always went crazy with the camera."

"I like her," Allison said thoughtfully.

"She likes you, too."

"I expected her to be…colder. After all, she did threaten to leave your family home to someone else, just because she doesn't like the women you date. That seems awfully judgmental to me."

Rick shrugged. "Yeah, she can be judgmental sometimes. But I'll always love Gran.

Three times in my life she's taken me in, no questions asked."

"What times?" Allison asked.

He glanced down at her. "What do you mean?"

"What times in your life did she take you in?"

He hesitated. "The first was when I was ten," he said after a moment. "My father had taken off, and my mother and I needed a place to stay while she got on her feet."

"Evie's your maternal grandmother? You have the same last name, so I assumed—"

"My mom went back to her maiden name after we came here, and I changed my name, too."

He remembered the day he'd put his father's name behind him forever. He also remembered living here, that first year. It had been like paradise. The first time in his life he'd ever felt safe. The first time he hadn't lain awake at night worrying about his mom, wondering when he'd be big enough and strong enough to protect her.

He shrugged away the memory. "The second time was when my mother got sick. I was sixteen, and I lived here while she was in the hospital. She died when I was seventeen, and I stayed here until I went away to college. The third time was after I came back from Afghanistan, before I settled in Des Moines and started Hunter Systems."

He glanced down at Allison again. She was looking at him with the quiet, thoughtful expression he remembered from the day at the hospital.

"Was it hard on you when your father left?" she asked.

"No," he said.

There was a foul taste in his mouth...the bitter flavor he associated with thoughts of his father. He wished the topic hadn't come up.

"Have you seen him since?"

"No."

On the other hand, maybe it was good to have a reminder of why he wasn't cut out for a real relationship. With his father's poison inside him, he didn't have any business getting serious with a woman.

Especially a woman like Allison.

He took a deep breath and looked away from her. There was silence between them for a moment, and Rick wasn't sure how to fill it.

"You two haven't gotten very far in that book yet."

He turned his head and saw his grandmother coming toward them with Meredith just behind her, carrying the Georgian tea tray.

"Allison, this is my grandmother's housekeeper, Meredith Bowen."

Meredith smiled at them both as she arranged the tea things with swift efficiency and drew up a chair for Gran.

His grandmother lifted the teapot and poured the amber liquid into three delicate china cups. "I hope you enjoy China black, Allison. Milk or sugar? Both? A girl after my own heart. Please help yourself to sandwiches and the miniature scones. We have Devonshire cream for those. And now you must tell me what you think of Hunter Hall."

"I think it's wonderful. I can see why Rick loves this place so much."

Gran smiled at her grandson. "I was always so happy whenever Richard came to stay. A house doesn't feel like a home without children. Speaking of children—"

Oh, no.

"What would you do if you lived in a place like Hunter Hall? Would you have a big family?"

"If I had a house like this?" Allison's eyes lit up, and Rick wondered what she was envisioning. He was pretty sure it wasn't giving birth to his children.

"If I had a house like this, I'd fill it with kids. Not my own, though," she added.

His grandmother looked startled.

"It's a dream of mine to open a retreat center for families dealing with childhood cancer," she explained.

"A retreat center?" his grandmother asked.

Allison nodded. "It's something I've thought about for years. A place that would provide services, and also create a sense of community for families. It's easy to feel isolated when you're struggling with cancer, because it's hard to explain what you're going through to people who've never dealt with it, and because hospital stays and treatment schedules don't leave you much free time. Megan's House would be a refuge. A place to go where everyone understands, because they're going through the same thing."

His grandmother looked interested. "What sort of services would you provide?"

Allison took a quick sip of tea and set her cup down again. "Families who live far away from Des Moines or other major hospitals could stay at the center while their children are in treatment, so they don't have to go to a hotel. There'd be day programs, too. Music and crafts and games for the kids. Therapy and counseling for the entire family. Massage and spa days for the moms…the dads too, if they need it. Parents forget to take care of themselves when their children are sick."

Her face was illuminated. "And there should be gardens. I grew up on a farm, and there's a kind of magic in being around growing things. Planting seeds and seeing them sprout, eating tomatoes right off the vine… I'd love for kids to be able to have gardens of their own, and lots of outdoor play spaces, too. Tree houses and clubhouses and—"

She stopped suddenly, blushing. "And that was me taking over the conversation to talk about myself. Wow. Sorry about that."

"You weren't talking about yourself," his grandmother said. "You were talking about a dream—something you want to build some-day."

She lifted the teapot carefully, one hand on the underside of the spout. Her eyes followed the flow of liquid as she refilled her cup. "I lost my daughter to cancer," she said.

Rick stared at her. He couldn't remember his grandmother ever mentioning his mother's death to someone outside the family.

"I know," Allison said softly. "Rick told me."

Gran looked up, and he could tell she was just as surprised as he had been.

"He did?"

Allison nodded. "I lost my sister Megan. She was fourteen when she died."

"Megan," his grandmother repeated. "Your center would be named after her?"

"Yes. Megan was full of life, and Megan's House would be, too. The way I imagine it, anyway," she added with a smile.

His grandmother sipped tea. "It's a wonderful dream, Allison. And I think you have the vision and persistence to achieve it. Now I understand why my friend Shirley Donovan speaks so highly of you. I must admit, I don't think I could bear to do what you do. Getting close to children when you know they won't all survive."

"That part is hard," Allison agreed. "My work isn't all gloom and sadness, though. I get to see strength and resilience and triumph, too. I consider myself lucky." She paused. "But that's enough serious conversation for one afternoon." She looked sideways at him. "I think we should change the subject to Rick's butt."

His grandmother's eyes widened. "Excuse me?"

Allison opened the photo album and handed it to her.

"Two naked pictures on the first page," Rick put in, shaking his head. "You're lucky I love you, Gran."

His grandmother was looking down at the album and trying, unsuccessfully, not to smile. "I'm sorry, Richard. I'd honestly forgotten these were in here. But you *were* an adorable little boy," she added.

"He was," Allison agreed, smiling at her.

They finished their tea with Evie quizzing Allison about her childhood. She asked about growing up on a farm, and Rick settled back against the sofa cushions to indulge in what was becoming a favorite pastime—watching Allison talk. When she was enthusiastic about something, her whole face lit up. Her hands sketched vivid gestures in the air. Her eyes sparkled, she leaned forward and she seemed to radiate energy.

"What is it?" she asked suddenly, looking at him. She'd just finished describing a typical day on the farm during planting season.

"I like watching you talk," he said honestly.

Allison blushed, and Rick felt Evie's eyes on both of them.

He cleared his throat. "We should probably think about heading out soon. Allison and I both have to work in the morning."

"Of course. I understand." His grandmother glanced at Allison. "I know it's early days, but—"

Oh, no.

"If you'd like, I can give you some pictures of Rick to take home with you. I have copies of all his childhood photos."

It could have been worse. With an opening like *it's early days, but*, she could have launched right into wedding plans.

"I'd love that," Allison said with a smile.

"Wonderful. I'll go and get them right now."

After she left Allison grinned at him. "Do you think I'll get copies of the naked ones?"

"Not if she values her life."

Allison laughed and picked up the album from the coffee table, laying it on her lap and starting to turn pages again.

He loved the way her short hair left her neck bare and exposed her delicate, shell-like ear. He imagined running the tip of his finger over the curve of that ear, and along the graceful line of her jaw, and over her lips.

His imagination had put his hands at her waist, sliding up under her sweater, before Allison spoke again.

"I thought your mom didn't get sick until you were sixteen?"

He frowned, surprised at the question.

She turned the album so he could see it,

and pointed to the picture that had caught her attention.

He shifted closer to look, and went still. He sensed rather than saw Allison watching him.

He remembered that picture of him and his mom. Gran had taken it the first day they'd come here to live.

"You both look so…tired," Allison said after a moment, as if searching for the right word.

That was one way to put it.

"Yeah," he said. He took in a deep breath and let it out again. "She wasn't sick yet, though. That picture…" he hesitated. "That's from when we came to live here, the first time."

There was compassion in her eyes. "After your father left?"

He nodded, watching her.

"Moving to a brand-new place, going to a new school…you must have been lonely."

He felt himself relax. The question she'd asked wasn't the one he had feared. "Not really. I was already into computers, which kept me busy. I started doing sports, too, after we moved here. And this house was like a paradise to me. So many places for a kid to explore. So fun, so safe—"

He stopped.

"Safe?" Allison asked after a moment. But then his grandmother came back into the room, saving him from having to answer.

"Here you go, my dear," Evie said with a smile, handing Allison a manila envelope that looked to be well stuffed with photos.

"Thank you so much. And thank you for that wonderful tea, and the tour. I had a lovely time."

"I had a lovely time, too. I do hope you'll come again."

"I'd like that," Allison said, smiling as she stood up. "Would you mind if I visit the powder room before I go?"

"Of course not. It's just through that doorway, down the hall on your left."

As soon as Allison was out of sight Gran turned on him.

"For all your faults, I never thought you were stupid."

He stared at her. "What?"

She was scowling at him. "A girl like Allison doesn't come along every day. I was so thrilled when I heard about the two of you… Shirley said the nicest things about her. She's a lovely girl, and it's obvious that you like her."

"Of course I like her. I'm dating her."

She swept right past that. "But what a way to show it! You're treating her like a friend, not a girlfriend—and that's where your relationship will end up. Honestly, there was a foot of space between you two all day."

"As you pointed out, Gran, Allison's not like the other girls I've dated. She'd not into public displays of affection."

"Oh, for goodness' sakes. I didn't expect her to sit in your lap. But you hold yourself apart from her, and it just about breaks my heart."

She shook her head. "I've had to watch you with a parade of bimbos over the years, and now that you've actually gotten a girl like Allison to go out with you, you're going to let her slip through your fingers. Sometimes I think—"

He was saved from hearing the rest of the harangue by the sight of Allison herself coming back into the room. As she came closer, looking sweet and fresh and achingly lovely, his hands twitched with the instinctive desire to touch her.

His grandmother was right about one thing. He did keep his distance from Allison, just as she kept hers from him. He'd given her space because he knew she preferred it that way—and because his attraction to her was borderline explosive, and there was no sense in playing with fire.

But now?

They said their final goodbyes at the front door and headed down the walkway toward his car. It was early evening, and the air was turning cool. The clouds in the western sky glowed with red and gold fire.

"So…how do you think it went?" Allison asked after a moment.

He didn't answer right away. His mind was churning, something he wasn't used to. Conflicting desires were wreaking havoc on his usually well-ordered emotions.

And yet there shouldn't be any conflict. The situation was simple. What he needed to do and what he wanted to do were one and the same.

The problem was, he wanted it too damn much.

"Rick? Do you think she bought our act?"

He looked down at her. She was smiling up at him, her eyes bluer than a summer sky, the sweetness in her a tangible thing. His gaze drifted to her lips, so soft and enticing.

One kiss. Just one.

He knew from experience that anticipation was usually better than reality. There was no way that kissing Allison could possibly live up to his vivid fantasies, and that might help take the edge off his desire.

He cleared his throat. "We didn't get rave reviews."

Her smile faded. "We didn't? But Evie liked me. At least I thought she did. And I liked her."

"Yeah, the two of you got along great. That's not the problem."

"Then what is?"

"I am. She doesn't think I…" He stopped. They'd reached the car, and he glanced back at the house. As he'd suspected, Evie was watching them through the living-room window.

He looked down at Allison again. She was watching him expectantly, waiting for him to finish his sentence.

She didn't have a clue what was on his mind right now.

He knew he should ask her first. Or at least warn her. But even though it made him a bastard, he wasn't going to do either of those things.

Instead, he took a step closer to her. Crossed the invisible barrier between them.

Her eyes widened as she took a step back, but his car was right behind her and she had nowhere to go.

She went still. Her lips parted as though she were about to speak, but no words came out.

He reached out and cupped the side of her face.

"You're so beautiful." He heard the rasp of

longing in his voice, felt the blood surging through his veins.

Then he kissed her.

Chapter Seven

The first touch of his lips was like an electric shock. Her knees buckled, and she would have fallen if he hadn't grabbed her by the waist.

His hands were like bands of steel, but his kiss was so soft…his mouth brushed over hers in a sweep of satin that made her whole body shiver.

Then he did it again. And again.

He kissed her like that until something inside her caught fire. Her hands went to his chest, her palms flat against his hard contours. She heard herself say his name in a trembling voice, a voice she hardly recognized.

He responded with a low growl. His hands slid around to her back, stroking up her spine to her shoulder blades, molding her to him. When her breasts flattened against his chest she gasped.

She could feel the air between them vibrating, humming, charged with something so magnetic it would only take the tiniest movement for them to be kissing again. If she shivered any harder…if her heart beat any faster…

She grabbed at the front of his shirt. Before she realized what she was doing, she tugged him closer.

He froze, and for a second *she* was the one kissing *him*, her mouth pressed to his.

Then he caught her in his arms and trapped her in the cage of his body.

His tongue pushed into her mouth and she opened to him eagerly. The kiss went from tender to demanding in the space of a heart-beat, the stroke of his tongue hot and possessive and unbearably erotic. Her very bones seemed to yield to him as she arched her back, rising up on her toes and locking her arms around his neck. She felt the sudden, hard thrust of his arousal against her stomach.

They broke apart at the same time.

She sagged back against the car, gasping for breath, unable to meet his eyes. She stared at his chest as she fought to recover, stunned at her reaction to him.

She felt dizzy, disoriented. Though she'd fantasized about Rick kissing her, none of her fantasies had prepared her for *this*.

"Your grandmother," she said after a minute, her voice sounding hoarse. She glanced at Hunter Hall, but if Evie had been at a window, she was gone now. "She was watching, wasn't she? That's why you…why you did that."

"She was watching, yeah." He paused. "But that's not why I did that."

Her hands curled into fists. Her heart, already racing, started to beat even faster.

"Allison."

Her eyes flew up to his face. His expression was fierce, eager, impatient.

"Come home with me tonight."

She stared at him. "What?"

"Come home with me."

Her face flamed. Should she be flattered that she'd graduated to the level of all his other women—good enough for a one-night stand?

She closed her eyes. The truth was, she couldn't blame Rick for assuming she'd jump into bed with him. She'd kissed him like she would. Like she wanted him more than air to breathe.

She felt his palm against her cheek, and she opened her eyes to meet his.

She took a deep breath. "Rick, I can't go home with you."

He dropped his hand, and she could see the eager light in his eyes fade a little. It killed her, because this was the side of Rick she'd been drawn to from the beginning, the one she'd always known was there. She was finally seeing the real, raw emotion he hid from the world.

But she wasn't fool enough to believe that one kiss from her had changed him, had turned him into a man who'd want more than one night or a few weeks from any woman. He'd been crystal clear about that from the beginning.

He was still breathing deep and hard. "Why?" He brushed his thumb across her lips, still swollen with his kiss. "I know you want me."

He trailed his fingers down the side of her neck, his eyes darkening when she quivered.

Yes, she wanted him. She wanted him with a wildness she'd never even imagined. She wanted him so much she ached with it.

Rick had broken through her fears and defenses to a part of her she hadn't known existed. But if she let him in any further, he'd break her heart. Already she cared for him much more than she should.

"I just want to go home," she said, trying to speak firmly but hearing her voice tremble. "Please take me home."

His hand dropped to his side and he took a step back. His expression was frustrated, disbelieving, and it occurred to Allison that women probably didn't turn him down very often.

Which was one of the reasons she couldn't do this. She couldn't become one of that faceless crowd, one of the thumbnail photos in *People*.

It would hurt too much.

"Okay," Rick said after a minute of silence, pulling his car keys out of his pocket. "Let's go."

The trip back seemed endless. Rick drove in silence, his eyes fixed on the road ahead. Allison kept her head turned away as she stared out the passenger window.

She'd seen his face when they'd first gotten into the car and she didn't want to see it again. His expression was so cold and remote it was easy to think she'd imagined it all—not just the heat when they kissed, but the warmth she'd seen in him during the ride over here, and at dinner last week, and when they'd visited Julie.

They pulled up in front of her building. She grabbed the door handle almost before the car stopped, but before she could open it, she felt Rick's hand on her shoulder.

She froze, and he dropped his hand

immediately. After a moment she twisted around to look at him.

"What?" she asked, wishing she could make her voice as cold and distant as he could make his.

"I'm sorry."

She waited, but he didn't say anything else. In spite of her determination to stay cool, her temper rose a little. "For what, exactly? Or is this a blanket apology?"

His jaw tensed. "I'm sorry for everything that happened after we said goodbye to my grandmother. Okay?"

Her temper rose further.

"Apology accepted." She reached for the door again.

"Damn it, Allison, wait a second. Give me a chance here."

"A chance to do what? You already apologized."

"Yeah, but you're still mad at me."

He sounded frustrated, but that, she decided, was not her problem. All she really wanted to do was get inside her apartment and run a hot bubble bath and try not to replay the kiss over and over in her head the way she had during the drive back.

"I'm sorry I kissed you. And I'm sorry things got…carried away." He paused. "You were right to turn me down when I asked you to come home with me. That would have been a mistake, for a lot of reasons."

And it would have, of course. But he sounded so cool when he said it.

She remembered the warmth in his voice when he told her she was beautiful. Was he even aware he'd said that to her? Or was that just part of his standard operating procedure?

She'd made the right decision. She knew she had. But for some reason, she suddenly felt like crying.

She took a quick breath. "It's not a big deal.

And your grandmother saw us, so it helped your cause. The sooner she believes in us, the sooner she'll give you Hunter Hall."

And the sooner she could have her normal life back.

He was silent for a moment. "You'll be relieved when it's over." It was a statement, not a question.

"A little," she admitted. She'd be sorry, too, but no good could come of admitting that. "I feel bad that we're lying to your grandmother. She has a good heart."

His eyes met hers. "I think if anyone can see into a person's heart, it's you. I hope you can look into mine and see that I really am sorry. That I would never deliberately hurt you."

Rick's heart. There were probably people out there who would swear it didn't exist.

She found herself thinking of a dozen different things. The kiss, Hunter Hall, the game he'd created in college. And then she thought of that picture in the album, the one that had bothered him so much.

His mother had looked thin and fragile and frightened, even with the smile she'd tried to put on for the camera. And Rick had been so fierce and protective as he stood beside her, trying to seem taller than he was, determined to be equal to anything the two of them had to face.

With the image of that boy in her mind, she looked again at the man he'd become—strong and powerful, successful and confident. And yet…when he'd first seen that picture, he hadn't looked confident at all. He'd looked the way he had that day in the hospital, reliving the loss of his mother.

Haunted. Vulnerable.

She thought of the father he wouldn't talk about, and the mother he'd lost. She thought of all the success he'd achieved as an adult, all his wealth, all his power.

She spoke without thinking, uttering something she'd never meant to say out loud. "Your heart is like an open wound."

His head jerked back as if she'd hit him. For a minute he just stared at her, his expression stunned.

She was a little stunned herself. "Rick, I'm sorry. I shouldn't have—I didn't mean—"

His jaw was tight. "Not a problem," he said. "Don't worry about it." He got out of the car and came around to her side, opening the door and standing back so she could get out. "Good night, Allison. Thanks for coming with me today."

She stepped out of the car and stood looking at him. "Good night," she said finally, unable to think of anything else to say. She started to walk toward her building, but when she heard his door slam shut and his engine start up, she turned back a moment to watch him drive away.

What had she been thinking? How could she have said something like that to a man like Rick Hunter?

Unless her subconscious had done it deliberately. Said something that the rich, powerful CEO would reject so completely he'd keep her at arm's length for the rest of their time together.

Because if the walls went up between them again, she wouldn't have to face the emotions churning inside her right now—the longing and regret and fear and desire that made her heart clench as she watched his car turn a corner and disappear from sight.

Maybe this was her way of running from those feelings. Or of driving Rick away.

If so, she'd done a damn good job of it.

It was a relief to be inside her apartment again. She took her favorite book into a hot bubble bath, and soaked until the water turned lukewarm. By the time she toweled off, put on pajamas and crawled into bed, she was starting to feel a little better. The bath had made her sleepy, and she started to drift off as soon as her head hit the pillow.

Then the phone rang.

She opened her eyes and glanced at the glowing digital numbers on her clock. Ten was a little late for a call on a Sunday night, but it was probably family.

"Hello?"

"Allison."

She was instantly awake, as if she'd rolled off the bed into ice water. Her hand tightened on the phone. "Rick?"

"Yeah. I'm sorry to call so late." He paused. "I hope I didn't wake you up."

"No, I…wasn't asleep."

"That's good." Another pause. This one went on so long she was about to check the phone connection when she heard his voice again.

"Allison, I need to see you. Just for a few minutes."

Here? Tonight? In her apartment? "Um…"

"Please."

She could hear the tension in his voice, and she knew she couldn't say no.

She sighed. "Okay."

"I'm downstairs right now. I can come up there, or we can go someplace for a drink if you'd rather."

Her heart thumped at the knowledge that he was so close.

"You can come up here. Give me a minute and I'll buzz you in."

"All right. And thanks."

Her pajamas were modest enough, but just to be safe, she put on a thick quilted robe and her oversized bunny slippers. Confident that she was sending no romantic signals whatsoever, she padded out to the living room and hit the buzzer.

A few moments later he was at her door.

The other advantage to her plaid armor was that it hid her body, which reacted to his presence in alarming ways. If she'd been wearing nothing but her thin cotton pajama top he would have seen her nipples harden for him, and that was a humiliation she could do without.

She stepped back to let him in. "Can I get you something to drink?"

"No, thanks." He followed her into the living room, hesitated a moment, and then took a seat on an armchair across from the couch.

Like her, he seemed to be avoiding anything that could be construed as a romantic signal.

She sat down on the sofa and cinched her robe a little tighter.

He leaned forward, his elbows on his knees and his hands clasped together. "I've been driving around the city for the past hour, until I ended up back here." He took a breath. "I'm so sorry for the way I acted tonight. And for leaving the way I did."

She shook her head. "I'm the one who should apologize. I had no right to say what I did. It was way too personal and—"

"It was true," he said, his voice harsh. "What you said was true. I just…didn't think anyone could see it. I'm like the wizard of Oz, telling people not to look at the man behind the curtain."

"Rick, you don't—"

"Let me finish. I don't know what it is about you that just…cuts through things. Maybe it's the work you do. If I dealt with cancer patients every day, with real pain and suffering, I'd be impatient with people's facades, too."

"Rick—"

"The funny thing is, I wanted the smoke and mirrors to work on you. I wanted to impress you. Even though what I like about you most is that you couldn't care less about money or power or any of that crap, even though it's childish and shallow, I still wanted you to be impressed. I sure as hell didn't want you feeling sorry for me."

"I've never felt sorry for you, Rick. Not once. That's the truth, and you have to believe me. I can see there's pain inside you, but that doesn't mean I pity you."

There was a silence. His eyes grew darker, and she knew he was revisiting old memories. After a moment she asked gently, "It's about your father, isn't it?"

"Yeah," he said, his voice sounding heavy. "It's about my father."

It was a long minute before he spoke again. "My mom fell in love with him when they were in high school. They ran off to get married, and even though my grandparents weren't exactly thrilled about it, they would have helped out. But my mom didn't want any help. She never cared about money, and she didn't want to shame my father by making it seem like he didn't have enough."

His head was bowed, and he looked down at his clasped hands as he spoke. "But he couldn't forget where she came from. I think he almost hated her for it. For having grown up with things he couldn't provide, even though she always told him she didn't care. He was convinced she'd leave him for another man, and he'd go into these jealous rages if my mom so much as talked to a neighbor or tipped the pizza delivery guy."

He took a deep breath. "I don't know if things were good in the beginning or not. By the time I came along, nothing was good. My father worked in construction, and he made decent money, but nothing like he thought he should be making. He started drinking, and… he started hitting my mom."

She'd known it was coming. Impossible *not* to know. But hearing him say it out loud made her heart twist in her chest, and she wanted to go to him so much it hurt.

But the best thing she could do for him right now was listen.

"He didn't hit me. He yelled at me a lot, but the one who got hurt was my mom. I think she…made it that way. She'd send me to my room if she heard a certain tone in my father's voice, or if he came home drunk.

"I was scared all the time. Not for myself, but for her. When I was eight or nine I started thinking about ways to protect her, but I was a scrawny little kid and my father was so big… I knew I couldn't fight him."

Allison felt a little sick. Parents were supposed to protect their children, not the other way around. But Rick hadn't had a childhood. You couldn't be a child when you were trying to protect your mother from your father.

"The year I turned ten I couldn't take it anymore. I was a little bigger, and I thought…I thought maybe I could at least get between them. He was getting worse, he hurt her bad enough to send her to the emergency room a couple of times. I was afraid he was going to kill her. So one night I tried. I came out of my room and got in the way, just like I'd planned. I woke up in the hospital."

He laughed, and the sound was so bitter she felt an ache at the back of her throat. "The funny thing is my plan actually worked. My father took off after that. He'd never actually hit me before, so maybe it freaked him out—or maybe he was scared about the consequences. Whatever the reason, we never saw him again.

"That's when we moved to Hunter Hall. I think my grandparents figured out some of what had happened, even though my mom never told them. But they got her to see a counselor, and they tried to make me go, too."

"You didn't?"

"No. I didn't want to talk about it. I just

wanted it over, done, in the past. I still want that. I've never wanted to see myself as a victim. As someone…damaged."

His words were like a hit to her solar plexus.

"Maybe that doesn't make sense to you," he said after a moment.

"You didn't want to be defined by what happened," she said, her voice shaking a little. "You didn't want to be defined by your father."

"That's it," he said. "That's it exactly. So I didn't go to counseling. I know I should have. I know I'd be better off now if I'd dealt with it then. But the only thing I wanted when I was a kid was to make sure no one could hurt me or my mom ever again. I started doing sports. When I was twelve I started lifting weights. I wanted to be bigger and stronger than my father, strong enough to protect my mom.

"And I did get strong. By the time I was sixteen I was big enough to stand up to anyone who might try to hurt her. I was going to protect her from everything, from ever feeling pain again."

He looked up then, and there was so much grief in his eyes that her heart broke. "And then she got cancer. I watched her suffer, and I couldn't help her." He swallowed convulsively. "It couldn't even kill her quick. It took her slow, piece by piece, until there wasn't anything left but the pain."

She was at his side before she could stop herself. She knelt on the floor and put her hands over his. They were like ice, and she willed her body's warmth to seep into him.

He took a deep breath. When he spoke again, she could hear the hopelessness in his voice. "All I wanted was to protect her. And in the end, the only thing I could do was watch while she died."

Her hands tightened around his. "But you tried. Even when you were a little boy, you tried to protect her." Something else clicked in her mind. "That's why you joined the military after 9/11. You wanted to do something to protect people."

"Don't say that. That makes me sound noble, and I'm not noble. I joined the military because I was young and reckless and—"

She shook her head. "I read a quote once, about soldiers putting their own bodies between their loved ones and the destruction of war. That's you, Rick. You're a protector. That's why I could never feel sorry for you."

He pulled his hands out of her grip, but only so he could cover hers, instead. His skin felt warmer now. "Didn't you hear what I've been saying? I've never been able to protect anyone. Maybe I tried when I was younger, but I never succeeded. And I sure as hell don't protect anybody now. I don't even care about anybody now."

"That's a load of crap," she said fiercely. "I've seen the list of charities your company supports. Educational grants for disadvantaged kids…mentoring programs…shelters for women and children. Don't you dare try to tell me you don't care. You care about your grandmother. You care about Julie, and you only met her last week."

There was a short silence. "Okay," he said, and for the first time she heard a hint of a smile in his voice. "Maybe I do care about a few people."

There was another silence, and Allison was aware, suddenly, of how intimate the space around them was. The only light in the room came from a small lamp on an end table. It cast a soft glow over them, while the rest of the room was in shadow.

It was so quiet she could hear Rick's breathing. It was so quiet she could hear her own heartbeat.

It felt like they were the only two people in the world.

She looked down at their joined hands. As she watched, his thumb started to move over her wrist, soft and slow.

She closed her eyes as heat bloomed inside her.

A minute like that, with nothing existing but his touch. Then he started to pull her toward him.

She wanted to follow where he led. She wanted to fall into his arms, to fall into *him*. But fear choked her, powerful and mindless, and she jerked away from his grasp before she could stop herself.

"It's getting late," she said, retreating back to the sofa. Her voice sounded strange, like it belonged to someone else.

"You're right," Rick said after a moment. "I should let you get some sleep."

He rose to his feet, and she rose with him. "Thanks for letting me see you," he said. "For letting me apologize. And…for the rest of it."

"All I did was listen."

He smiled a little. "You did more than that."

His words warmed her. "I was glad to do it."

There was another pause, and they looked at each other.

It would be so easy to lose herself in those green eyes. Her furled edges seemed to open toward him, like a flower opening to the sun.

"Of course, you realize this doesn't change anything between us."

Her heartbeat quickened. "What do you mean?"

"Our bargain," he reminded her. "Until Hunter Hall is mine, you're still on the hook."

She should have known that's what he meant. "Right. Yes. Of course."

"We should make plans for next weekend. Any ideas?"

He sounded almost businesslike, and she tried to focus. "Well. Are you still willing to meet my family?"

"Absolutely. In fact, that would be perfect. I'll make sure my grandmother knows about it. That combined with the show we put on today should convince her that I'm serious about you. What do you have in mind?"

"There's a birthday party at my parents' farm next Saturday. For Jake and Jenna, my brother and sister. They're twins. Jake will only be there via video, since he's in Afghanistan, but Jenna and a sizeable chunk of the Landry clan will be in attendance."

"Count me in."

She took a quick breath. "Okay, then. I'll let everyone know you'll be there."

It occurred to her that she'd be introducing Rick to her parents for the first time. To her whole family, in fact.

She couldn't help wondering what he'd think of them. And what they'd think of him.

Rick moved toward the door, and she followed. He paused with his hand on the knob.

"Good night, Allison."

"Good night, Rick."

He smiled at her briefly, and then he was gone.

She closed the door after him. When she realized she was still standing there a minute later, listening to the sound of the elevator taking him back downstairs, she turned away.

She went back into the living room, but she was too restless to sit down. She paced back and forth instead, her eyes unseeing, her hands stuck deep in the pockets of her robe.

She was falling for Rick Hunter.

And even though this was the first time she'd acknowledged the truth, she knew in her heart she'd been falling for him from the moment they'd met.

But nothing had really changed. They were still the same people, with the same problems.

He'd told her things tonight she was sure he'd never told anyone else, but that didn't change who he was. Rick wasn't suddenly going to start believing in the possibility of happiness or love, or anything outside himself.

Except for Hunter Hall, of course. That, he could believe in. The house had been his haven, his sanctuary, and it had the advantage of being made of stone instead of flesh and blood.

She understood better now why he wanted it so much, why he'd go to any lengths to make sure it was his. And she'd carry out her side of their bargain, and do everything she could to get Rick the one thing in the world he would ever let himself want.

Not that he didn't want her. She was pretty sure that whatever Rick felt toward her now, it included a healthy dose of want. But even if that could be enough for her, she still had her own walls to contend with. Walls that were still firmly in place.

Allison went over to the window and rested

her forehead against the cool glass. She'd been perfectly happy with her life until Rick had come along. He'd turned her well-ordered existence upside down.

And no matter how hard she worked to put it all back together, she knew her heart would never be the same.

Chapter Eight

On Monday Rick went down to the third floor to touch base with his VP of product development.

"What are you doing in this part of the building?" Derek asked. "It's been weeks since you visited R&D. I thought you didn't give a damn what we design any more, as long as it makes money."

That shot hit home, and he remembered what Carol had said. Was he really turning into a corporate suit?

"I know I've been focusing on business

products lately, but I was thinking about getting back into game design. And I know you've been making noises about educational software…"

Derek looked astonished. "You're actually going to look at my product proposal? I thought you said the profit margins would be too low to make it worthwhile."

"I'd just like to explore a few ideas. I'm having the sales group compile some market data. I thought you and I could have a brainstorming session on the products themselves."

Derek grinned at him. "If you think you can keep up with me. How long has it been since you've written code, old man?"

"I could run circles around you."

"And what about this game idea? What's the theme going to be?"

"Warrior women. A lot of our gaming products have a male focus, so I thought it might make sense—commercially speaking—to go after the female demographic, as well."

Derek raised an eyebrow. "You never worried about the female demographic before, and you always swore you'd never go back to design. What brought this on?"

Allison had brought it on—but he wasn't about to admit that.

She was the reason he'd started thinking about educational software, because it would help kids. And she was the reason he'd woken up at four o'clock that morning with game ideas flying around his brain. Being with her had shaken something loose inside him, and the creativity he'd thought was long dead seemed to be flowing again.

He shrugged. "Nothing in particular. And the game is just in the nascent stages, the creative fog phase. Maybe nothing will come of it."

"Something will come of it. And I think

I'll be sending Allison a big fruit basket later today."

Rick frowned. "I didn't say anything about Allison."

Derek grinned. "I know you didn't."

He thought about calling her a dozen times that day, but resisted temptation. They were both busy people and he didn't want to push.

He told himself the same thing on Tuesday. By Wednesday, he was running out of will-power.

Whenever he thought about their kiss, his body hardened—and he thought about it a lot.

He couldn't remember the last time a single kiss had affected him this much. It was as if his world had shifted on its axis, reorienting itself around that one moment.

He'd gone to her apartment that night to apologize, and ended up telling her things he never thought he'd tell a living soul. Her warmth and compassion had almost undone him, but it was that bulky robe and her ridiculous bunny slippers that had made him want to kiss her again.

He'd started to, but she'd pulled away from him fast. That was the Allison he knew—protective of her space, wary of physical contact.

Only now he knew another side of her, too. A woman who came alive in his arms. A woman who kissed with a passion that left him shaking, and aroused him more than any woman he'd ever known.

A woman he was determined to be with, even if it was just for a little while.

He knew she deserved more. Allison deserved a man who could be a husband and a father, a man who would love her for the rest of her life.

But even though she deserved it, she wasn't looking for it—at least not right now. She'd said so herself.

Which meant there was no reason the two of them couldn't be together.

He'd be breaking his cardinal rule of dating, of course. He didn't get involved with women he could care about. But it would only be for a few weeks, maybe a few months. And no woman had ever tempted him the way Allison did.

She'd turned him down once, but he'd propositioned her with all the finesse of a randy teenager. It had been too much, too fast—especially after a kiss that had knocked them both for a loop.

And Allison had been single for a long time, with every intention of staying that way. He couldn't push her into a relationship the way he'd pushed her into that kiss.

But he could sure as hell try to persuade her.

His cell phone rang, and he flipped it open absently.

"Rick?"

A jolt went through him.

"It's Allison," she added, as if he couldn't have told her voice from the voice of every other woman on the planet.

"I was just thinking about calling you," he said. "To see when you wanted to leave on Saturday."

"I was calling you for the same reason."

He leaned back in his chair. "Great minds think alike. So what time should I pick you up?"

"I'd like to drive this time. I tried to imagine your Porsche in my parents' driveway, and I just couldn't do it."

"You're such a reverse snob." He turned his chair toward the window and caught sight of his reflection, smiling back at him. "So what do you drive?"

"A secondhand pickup."

"Of course you do. You're just an Iowa farm girl at heart, aren't you?"

"Smile when you say that, city boy."

He knew exactly what she looked like right now—her eyes glinting with mischief, her mouth quirked up at the corners.

"I look forward to being chauffeured to your parents' farm in your secondhand truck. Is it red?"

"Blue."

"To match your eyes?"

"Of course. I'm sure you've noticed how good I am at accessorizing."

He was almost glad she wasn't there in person, to see him grinning like a fool. "What time should we leave?"

"Um…noon? And I warn you, this is a Landry party and it could go on for hours. I almost feel guilty for subjecting you to this."

"Are you kidding? I wouldn't miss it. But speaking of subjecting people to things…"

"Uh-oh."

"It's not so bad. My company's charity ball is next weekend. Great food and a great band, and you'll get to see me in a tux. Sound good?"

"Does the fact that you're asking mean I don't have to go?"

He raised an eyebrow, even though she wasn't there to see it. "Sorry. This event is definitely required under the terms of our agreement, since there's no way my girlfriend wouldn't be there with me."

"Maybe your girlfriend could have an attack of the flu? I have to say, black tie and dancing aren't exactly my thing."

"Are you trying to weasel out of our deal? I'm surprised at you, Allison. You seem so much more honorable than that."

"I see you're determined to get your pound of flesh."

"Just making sure you hold up your end of our bargain."

"Maybe I'll show up in jeans, just to annoy you."

He could hear the smile in her voice, and he wanted to drive over to her office right now, so he could see it in person. "No jeans allowed, Ms. Landry. Evening attire is mandatory."

"Hmm. I think I'll buy a dress in a nice shade of puce, with a big orange sash and a matching feather boa."

"I'll bring smelling salts in case I need to be revived from the shock. And I'm looking forward to meeting your family this weekend."

"That's only because you have no idea what you're getting into."

"You're not going to scare me off, Allison. I'll see you Saturday at noon."

Carol came in a few minutes later, as he was reviewing Derek's product presentation.

"You look cheerful," she said. "Got something fun planned for tonight?"

"For Saturday."

"Yeah? What?"

"I'm going to meet Allison's family. And next weekend she's coming with me to the charity ball."

Carol was silent, and he glanced up after a moment to see her grinning at him.

"What?" he asked suspiciously.

"Rick and Allison, sitting in a tree—"

"Cut it out, Carol."

"I just never thought I'd see the day, that's all. In all seriousness, boss, it's nice to see you so happy. Keep it up."

She left before he could say anything else.

"You were right," Rick said forty-eight hours later. "I had no idea what I was getting into."

It was a gorgeous April afternoon, the sky an endless blue, the air alive with the scents of springtime. Here on the Landry farm there was a restless, joyful urgency everywhere, in the huge farmhouse kitchen where dozens of people were talking, laughing and cooking, and out in the fields where there was work to be done, party or no party.

Allison had taken him outside to meet her father, and somehow that had led to him sitting in a low metal seat hitched behind a tractor, with Allison sitting in an identical seat next to him. Between them were two large trays of tomato plants. Allison's father was on the tractor seat, twisted around so he could give them instructions.

"So you understand what you're supposed to do, right? I'm going to drive across the field making holes in the turf, and you're going to grab the plants and stuff them in the holes. Be gentle with the roots, but quick. Got it?"

"Uh…"

"Great," Joe Landry said, turning back around and starting up the tractor.

"Don't worry," Allison said, grinning at him. She was wearing an Iowa Hawkeyes baseball cap and she had a smudge of dirt on one cheek. "You'll get the hang of it."

She grabbed two plants from the tray and held them out. He took them gingerly.

"They're not made of glass," she said. "Gentle but quick, remember? Okay, here we go."

"Ready?" Joe called out over the rumble of the tractor.

"Ready!" Allison called back.

The tractor started to roll.

Half an hour later Rick was covered in dirt and the spicy scent of young tomato plants. They'd planted several dozen rows, with Allison's sister Jenna replacing the trays every time they crisscrossed the field.

"Good job!" Joe called out, grinning at them

as he turned off the tractor and jumped to the ground. "Dinner's in an hour and a half, kids. Allison, why don't you show Rick around the place?"

"Sounds like a plan," Allison agreed, rising quickly and gracefully to her feet while Rick extricated himself from the low seat a little more slowly.

"Would you guys mind if I join you?" Jenna asked. "I forgot what it's like to have the whole family milling around in the kitchen, and I need a break before I go back in there."

Allison laughed. "Is that why you volunteered for tomato duty?"

"Pretty much."

"My sister lives in Chicago and missed the last few family gatherings," Allison explained, and something clicked in Rick's mind.

"Jenna Landry," he said, snapping his fingers, and looking at Allison's sister with new respect. "You were lead guitarist for the Red Mollies."

Jenna, a tall, dark-haired beauty with Allison's blue eyes, cocked her head at him. "I'm impressed," she said. "I wouldn't have pegged you for the indie rock type."

Rick grinned at her. "Actually, an army friend of mine had a huge crush on you. He listened to 'Runaway Heart' every night before he fell asleep."

Jenna winked at him. "I bet it gave him good dreams," she said in the husky voice that had probably haunted the dreams of thousands of men.

"Don't practice your wiles on him," Allison admonished her sister, brushing dirt off her jeans. "He'll fall hopelessly in love with you, like they all do, and then you'll break his heart."

The three of them started to walk down the path beside the tomato patch, toward the fenced in pasture behind the barn. There was something invigorating about the scent of freshly turned earth in the fields on either side of them. The promise of summer was like a kiss against his skin.

"How about it?" Jenna asked, drawing his arm through hers. "Are you up for having your heart broken?"

The nice thing about having Jenna on one arm was that it gave him an excuse to offer his other arm to Allison. She took it, and her warmth seemed to radiate through him as they made their way toward the barn.

"Let's see if I survive today before I put my heart on the chopping block. Do you always put your party guests to work?"

"Only the ones we like," Allison said, grinning up at him under the brim of her baseball cap. "You should take it as a compliment. Dad doesn't trust just anyone with his precious tomatoes."

"I'm surprised he didn't take the day off, to enjoy the party."

Allison shook her head. "There speaks someone who wasn't raised on a farm. There's no time off in the spring. Winter is our time to relax. But he's done for the day—out here, anyway. Now he'll shower and change and Mom will put him to work in the kitchen."

They reached the fence, and the three of them leaned against the top rail to look out at the grassy expanse of the pasture.

"What's this used for?" he asked, just as a brown horse came into view, trotting purposefully toward them. His black mane and tail rippled like silk.

"There's my beauty," Allison said in a voice he'd never heard her use before. He glanced down at her, startled, to see her taking a handful of sugar cubes out of her pocket. She put them into her baseball cap and held it out. The horse nosed into the cap and tossed his sleek brown head after he finished the treat.

"Remember when you used to ride Merlin bareback? I dare you to do that right now," Jenna challenged her, and Rick saw the sibling dynamic assert itself between the two women.

"I could do it with my eyes shut," Allison said loftily, grinning at her sister.

"Less talk and more action. I double dare you."

Allison handed Rick her baseball cap and climbed the fence, balancing herself against the top rail as she ran a caressing hand along the animal's proud neck. He wore neither saddle nor bridle.

"Uh…Allison? Are you sure this is really a good—"

She wasn't listening to him as she threaded her fingers into the horse's mane, climbed to the top of the fence, and threw her leg over his back. She seemed to whisper something into his ear and the two of them were off across the field, the horse cantering and Allison laughing as she hung on with her hands and her knees.

Rick stared after them. They seemed to be in perfect harmony, the two of them alike some-how in their fearless, joyful grace. He'd never seen her like this—so exuberant, so confident in her physicality.

So sexy.

"She's the most beautiful woman I've ever seen," he said under his breath, remembering the second the words were out of his mouth that he wasn't alone.

He glanced down at Jenna. "Is there any chance I didn't say that out loud?"

"Nope." She was staring at him, wide-eyed. After a moment she grinned and pointed a finger at him. "You've got a crush on my little sister," she said.

He thought about denying it, but who was

he kidding? The fact was, he did have a crush on Allison.

"It's possible," he admitted. "But I haven't been making a lot of progress."

"It's not personal. I mean…Allison doesn't date. You know that, right?"

"Yeah, I know that," Rick said, resting his forearms on the top rail of the fence. "But I don't know why."

Jenna shook her head. "I don't know, either. We're close in a lot of ways, and I love her with my whole heart, but you've probably figured out that Allison doesn't like talking about herself. She's always made her life about other people. Whenever I ask her about it, she's tells me she'd rather focus on work."

"That's what she told me, too."

Rick looked toward the pasture again. Horse and rider were far across the field. "What was she like in high school?"

"A lot like she is now, although I'm ashamed

to say I wasn't around much when Allison was a teenager. I left home when I was eighteen, and she was fifteen."

"You left because of your music?"

"That's right. What a cliché, huh? I used to think of it like a headline: 'Rebellious Teen Leaves Home To Start Rock Band.'"

"You made a success of it. The Red Mollies were huge for a while."

Jenna shrugged. "We put out some good music, anyway. I loved writing songs, loved being on the road and doing shows… It's what I'd dreamed of my whole life. But I always felt guilty that I wasn't here more for Allison and my parents when Megan got sick. She got diagnosed about a year after I left. My brother Jake had joined the army and was stationed down in Georgia, so he couldn't get home much. I came back every month or so, but I could have done a lot more. I could have taken a break from the band to be here for my family."

"Your band was probably like family, too. You didn't want to leave them in the lurch."

"That was part of it, sure. But if I'm being honest with myself...well, the reality is I let Allison carry a burden I should have made lighter for her. I didn't realize how much she would give up, to be the person everyone could count on."

Rick glanced at her sharply. "Give up? What did she give up?"

Jenna rested her elbows on the fence rail.

"She had this boyfriend, a guy who went to school with her. Allison went to Fisher Academy, did you know that? On a full academic scholarship. She was always crazy smart, always at the top of her class. We were so proud when she got into Fisher. It wasn't easy for her, either. Those rich kids didn't exactly make her feel welcome. That's why we were so surprised when she started dating one of them."

He was trying to stay focused on what Jenna was saying but he was dealing with an unwelcome rush of emotion. Was he actually feeling jealous of Allison's high school boyfriend? God, how pathetic could he get? "What was his name? The boyfriend, I mean."

"Paul, I think. Allison was crazy about him. You know, the way a teenage girl is crazy about her first love."

"Sure," Rick said. Another pulse of jealousy made his jaw tighten. He wished he could have known Allison back then, when she was capable of feeling like that. She was so different, now—so self-contained, so determined not to give herself away. "What happened to Mr. Wonderful?"

"Allison broke up with him. She never talked about why, and my parents were pretty focused on Megan at the time, so I don't think they worried too much about it. I always wondered if maybe…"

"What?"

"If maybe she broke up with him because of Megan. So she could focus all her time and energy on her, and on my Mom and Dad. So she could take care of her family."

Was that what had happened? Was that the reason Allison didn't date now—because she'd fallen in love once and let the guy go? Was she still carrying a torch for her high school sweetheart?

Allison was coming back toward them now and he had a sudden urge to grab hold of her and kiss her, as if he could force love out of the depths of her soul.

Love?

No, not love. That was too big a word, too big a feeling…and something he had no business even thinking about. The rush of possessiveness he'd felt just now was proof of that.

His father had been possessive and jealous, full of rage and hate. Rick's determination to escape that bitter legacy meant he'd never be husband or father material. There was no way he'd risk putting any woman through what his mother had been through.

So he would never take a chance on forever. But he wanted Allison, wanted her to be his for a few weeks or a few months. He wanted her in his bed, giving him her sweetness and warmth and passion and desire.

He hated knowing that she'd felt that way for someone else, so many years ago—and that she'd locked those emotions away forever. Locked away her heart so that no man could ever touch it again.

Allison maneuvered the horse back to the fence and dismounted neatly and gracefully.

"Wow, that felt good," she said, sitting on the top rail and grinning down at them both. "Sorry I deserted you there for a while. Did you make any progress with Rick?" she asked her sister.

Jenna shook her head. "Nope. He's a hard nut."

"Well, I'm glad to hear it. He deserves better than to get his heart stomped on by the likes of you."

She looked so beautiful sitting there with that smudge of dirt on her face, her blue eyes a shade darker than the sky. He loved the way the sunlight made her brown hair gleam with gold, and he loved the way her small, firm breasts filled out her T-shirt. Before he could stop himself he reached up and brushed her cheek with the pad of his thumb.

She froze, her eyes wide and startled.

"Dirt," he said, his voice a little rough. He cleared his throat. "You had a smudge of dirt on your cheek."

She was staring at him, her lips parted.

"I think I'll head inside and check on my birthday cake," Jenna said into the sudden, charged silence, and Rick was vaguely aware that she had left them, walking briskly back toward the house.

His eyes didn't leave Allison's as he put his hands on her waist. He intended to help her jump down from the fence, but instead he moved closer and let his hands slide up her torso, slowly, just brushing the outside of her breasts. Then he did hoist her off the fence, setting her carefully on her feet.

Her cheeks were red and her breath was coming faster than usual, but she was meeting his eyes and she didn't shy away. He looked down at her, not kissing her the way he wanted to, not moving a muscle.

He wasn't pushing, and she wasn't running.

It felt like a beginning. And as he fell deeper into her blue eyes, Rick realized that he wanted more than Allison's passion.

He wanted her trust. And he was willing to do whatever it took to earn it.

Chapter Nine

Allison had never felt so grateful for the cheerful, noisy chaos of her family. She knew Rick was coming in behind her as she pushed through the screen door into the kitchen, but since they'd already done introductions when they first arrived, she didn't need to say anything but hello in answer to the chorus of greetings.

She saw her cousin Ben, a freshman in college, collar Rick and start talking to him eagerly. She was pretty sure an impassioned conversation about "Magician's Labyrinth" was underway. She was glad to be able to lose herself in the cluster of people around the big table, nibbling on the appetizers her mother had set out for everyone.

After only a minute or two, though, she looked for him again. He and Ben were talking over by the counter. Rick turned his head and their eyes met. She flushed and looked away.

Something in his expression made her feel a little dizzy.

It wasn't the fevered desire she'd seen at Hunter Hall. This was…well, she couldn't put her finger on exactly what it was, but it made her feel languid and restless at the same time, a combination of feelings she'd never experienced before.

Thank God she was talking with Aunt Beth, so all she had to do was listen and nod at appropriate moments. Her heart was thumping and her skin felt warm.

She saw out of the corner of her eye that her dad had approached Rick and captured his attention, and she couldn't help feeling curious about their conversation. She said something vague to Aunt Beth, who turned her attention to someone else, and Allison moved closer to where her dad and Rick were sitting at the kitchen table.

Rick looked comfortable in worn jeans and a short-sleeved polo shirt. His black hair had started the day off neat but had long since taken on the tousled look she preferred. She wished she could run her fingers through it, brush it off his forehead. She wished she could touch him the way he'd touched her outside, easy and knowing and sensual.

Allison drifted a little closer, and overheard them talking about community supported agriculture, of all things. Rick turned his head and met her eyes again.

"Hey," he said, smiling and holding out his hand.

After just a second's hesitation she took it, and as Rick tugged her closer so she could be part of the conversation, she knew he couldn't possibly realize what a big deal this was for her. Just to take a man's hand like this, letting her nervousness crackle across her skin without letting it stop her. To move through the anxiety, the self-doubt, and to even tighten her hand around his a little, as if to affirm that she was choosing this contact, this link, to a man she knew was more than a friend to her.

But for this moment, she didn't need to define what Rick was in her life. She was holding his hand, and that was enough.

She realized her father had asked her something.

"What?"

"I said you should be the one to tell Rick how CSA works. Considering you were the one who helped us implement it here."

It was hard to focus with her awareness so centered on her right hand, with Rick's warm, strong fingers wrapped around hers.

"Okay. Sure." She took a deep breath. "I actually researched the CSA business model my senior year in college, and I loved it so much I convinced my parents to redesign their marketing strategy around it."

"She's pretty persuasive," Joe said with a smile.

"So says a fond parent. Anyway, if you're a customer, you buy a share in your local farm's growing season. A big family might buy two shares. In return, you get a box of fresh vegetables every week. It's a great system for farmers because they can do sales and marketing during the slow winter months, so by the time things get crazy in the spring and summer they've already sold their year's worth of produce. And because they receive the money up front, cash flow is more predictable."

She began to warm to her topic, because this was one of the things she was passionate about. "It's really a wonderful program. Farmers get to know their customers; the people in a community get to know their local farms. There's shared risk, too. If heavy rains wash away a crop one week, everyone's disappointed together. If there's a bumper crop of strawberries or tomatoes or corn, everyone benefits. You feel more connected to what's happening locally with the weather and the land, and of course you get fresh, seasonal produce every week, which makes for a healthy diet."

"You're right, she is persuasive," Rick said, turning to her father. "Is it too late in the season to buy a share?"

"Sorry," Joe said. "Thanks to Allison's help—she set up a website for us a few years ago, among other things—we usually sell out by the end of January. But we can put you on the waiting list for next year."

"I'd like that."

Joe asked Rick a question about his business, and at the same time Rick started stroking the back of her hand with his thumb. It was the smallest movement, featherlight on her skin, but she was glad that the two men could carry on the conversation by themselves for a few minutes, because that small movement was all she could think about.

But she didn't feel an urge to pull away, to run and hide. She stayed right where she was, letting wave after wave of sensation radiate through her body, feeling warm and giddy and alive.

In spite of her preoccupation, one thing Rick said caught her attention.

"Did you say Hunter Systems is going to expand into educational software?"

"That's right. I've got a VP with some fantastic ideas. We may be ready to put the first products on the shelves as early as next year."

"Rick, that's wonderful! You're lucky to have the power to make something like that—something that will help children learn. I'm so—" she stopped abruptly.

"You're so what?" he prodded. He shifted his hand so he could lace his fingers through hers, and a fresh wave of goose bumps prickled her skin.

"I was going to say, proud of you. But that sounds patronizing."

He shook his head. "No, it doesn't."

"I think I heard you tell Ben you're designing a new game?" her father asked.

"That's right," Rick said. "Of course it's only in the beginning stages at this point…"

"Rick! Are you serious? You're creating something new?" Somehow, this made her even happier than the news about the software line. She squeezed his hand, and he smiled at her. "I thought you'd be happy about that," he said softly.

The warmth in his eyes was making her feel a little light-headed. "I can't wait to see the new game," she said.

She thought she knew why Rick had stopped designing after "Magician's Labyrinth." As he got older, he moved further and further away from anything that might make him feel. He didn't trust emotion, whether good or bad. And creating something was definitely an emotional process.

He was letting himself create again. Did that mean he was ready to let other emotions in, too?

"Dinner's ready!" her mom called out, and her dad went to help as people sorted themselves out around the big table.

"Where should I sit?" Rick asked, letting go of her hand at last.

"Next to me," Allison said.

"My favorite place." He gave her a quick, private grin that made her heart beat faster.

She was aware of him all through dinner, as he talked with various members of her family and tucked away an impressive amount of chicken and stuffing and vegetables. When the meal was over and the table had been cleared her cousin Kate set up a laptop with a webcam on the table, and Allison forgot Rick for the first time all day when the face of her older brother came up on the screen.

"Hey, everybody," Jake said with the old grin she remembered, even though his face looked worn and tired.

"Happy Birthday!" they all called out, and her mom brought out an enormous cake with *Jake and Jenna* spelled out in homemade frosting. Jenna blew out the candles for both of them, and then everyone started talking at once.

"Pipe down," Irene said after a few minutes. "Did I hear that right, Jake? You're really coming home for good?"

"Yeah, sometime this fall," Jake said. "My commitment is up and I'm getting out."

There was a chorus of cheers and excited talk, but Allison was quiet. There was something in Jake's eyes that worried her. He'd deployed to Iraq three times and was in Afghanistan now, but this was the first time she'd seen his expression look so shuttered, so shadowed.

Beside her, Jenna was quiet, too. When Allison met her eyes she knew her sister had seen the same thing she had.

"He'll be home soon," she said softly, putting her arm around Jenna's waist. Her sister nodded, leaning against her for just a minute before it was time to say goodbye to their brother. He blew them a kiss, and then the screen went blank.

After they'd eaten their cake the family drifted into the living room, breaking into smaller groups for conversation. Her dad acted as the bartender, filling drink orders for anyone who wanted anything, and the musical members of the family gravitated together as they always did, starting an informal jam session over by the piano. Allison saw Jenna relax a little once she had her guitar in her hands, and she went back into the kitchen where a few people lingered to wash dishes, including her mother and Rick.

They were side by side at the kitchen sink, Rick washing and her mother drying. Allison paused in the doorway to watch them, a slow smile spreading across her face.

"We really are putting you to work today," she said after a minute.

They both turned their heads, and Rick gave her that grin again, the one that made her stomach muscles tighten. "Bring this one to dinner anytime," her mother said. "Willing dishwashers are always welcome. But I understand you owe Rick a look at our photo albums."

Allison started to laugh. "That's right! I forgot. You really want to look through Landry family history?"

"Of course I do."

Irene shooed them both toward the door. "The albums are upstairs in your dad's study," she said, turning back to the sink.

A few minutes later Rick was sitting beside her on the old leather sofa as they flipped through photos that Allison hadn't looked at in years.

"Oh, my God," she said for the tenth time, laughing at the sight of herself in braces, the worst haircut she'd ever had and her junior-high soccer uniform.

"You're adorable in this picture," Rick said.

"I'm hideous!"

"Adorable."

She shook her head at him and turned the page. Her mother had put several pictures of Megan together here, collage style.

"You used this one in your memoir," Rick said, pointing at Megan's seventh-grade school photo.

"You read my memoir?"

He nodded. "I read it last week," he said. "Why do you sound so surprised?"

She thought about it. Why did it surprise her so much? "Well, you stayed away from hospitals for almost twenty years after your mother died. I guess I thought you avoided the subject of cancer in general."

"Yeah, I do. But I didn't read your book because it was about cancer. I read it because you wrote it. I'm interested in you, in case you haven't figured that out."

"Oh." She felt warm all over, and she found herself admitting something she hadn't meant to. "I bought 'Magician's Labyrinth' last week. I've been playing it at home, after work."

It was his turn to look surprised.

"I didn't think you liked video games."

"I don't, usually. But it's like what you said about my book. You made it, so I'm interested in it."

He grinned at her, and the warmth inside her deepened. "So what's your verdict? Do you like it?"

"I didn't think I would."

"But you do?"

"I love it! I'm completely addicted. A couple of nights ago I played for two hours straight."

He laughed out loud, and Allison couldn't help laughing with him. He had a great laugh, big and deep and contagious.

"What about my book?" she asked, curious to know his opinion. "What did you think of it?"

"I thought it was amazing. But it did make me wonder about the parts you left out."

She stared at him. "What do you mean, left out?"

He reached for one of the other albums on the coffee table—one she hadn't planned to show him. Her mother had written dates on the covers, and she knew this one would have photos of her junior and senior year at Fisher Academy, a time in her life she didn't particularly want to remember.

"Your book was so brave. You didn't hold anything back—about Megan, anyway. About what she went through, and what you and your family went through while she was sick, and when you lost her."

He'd opened the album, and was flipping slowly through it. "But you didn't talk about yourself outside of Megan. You were a teenager—there must have been other things going on in your life. Things that didn't have anything to do with Megan, or your family."

"The book was about Megan, not me. She was important. My family was important," Allison said, her voice tight as Rick turned pages. "I don't—"

There it was, on the next page. Her junior prom picture.

There were probably several more pictures of her and Paul in this album. Years ago she'd thought about taking them out, but she'd been afraid her parents would notice. She'd been so successful at avoiding questions…she hadn't wanted to do anything that would risk the precarious balance she'd found for herself.

She looked down at her lap, and saw her hands clenched into childish fists, her thumbs tucked inside as if she were trying to protect something.

"What happened?" Rick asked, his voice soft.

"What do you mean?"

"Just now. You were relaxed and laughing, and now you're not. Won't you tell me, Allison?"

"Tell you what?"

"Why this guy still has such a hold on your heart."

"Is that what you think?" she asked, grateful that he was so far from the truth.

She took a deep breath and let it out slowly, forcing herself to glance at the picture. Paul was looking relaxed and confident and handsome, and she looked…young. Young and innocent and happy, and the sight made her feel so helpless, and then so angry, that she stretched her hands out and made fists again—the right way, this time.

"This isn't something I talk about," she said.

"Why not?"

"Because it's not important."

He closed the album with more force than necessary and dropped it on the coffee table. "What's not important? You?"

He got up and paced around the room, dragging a hand through his black hair. Allison's emotions were a tight, unhappy knot inside her.

"Rick, I'm—" She took a deep breath. "I'm not ready for this," she heard herself say. "Not yet."

He stopped pacing and stared at her. After a moment, he came over to the coffee table and sat down on the edge of it, facing her. Their knees were almost touching.

"You're not ready yet. But…someday?"

His eyes were intense. She looked down, unable to meet them. She knew what he was really asking her.

Her breath was stuck in her throat. Her lungs ached, but she couldn't seem to take a full breath. "I don't know," she said after a moment, her voice so low she wasn't sure he'd be able to hear her.

"You don't know?" he repeated.

She looked up at him again. The knot inside her loosened, and instead she felt the low, coiling warmth that had teased at her for the last few hours.

His face had become so familiar to her. The black hair falling over his forehead, the green eyes under dark brows, the shadow of stubble on his jaw. She could read tension in his face, and in the muscles of his arms and shoulders. She remembered him helping her down from the fence and setting her on her feet, the same strain in every line of his body.

His tension made him hard as stone, power leashed in every muscle, while hers had the opposite effect. She felt herself softening, unraveling, her very bones melting. She wanted to touch him, to press the curves of her body against the hardness of his, to see if the tension in him eased or turned into something else.

"I want to be," she said. Her face flooded with color, as if she'd propositioned him.

"You do?" His voice was soft, but there was heat in his gaze.

Her heart slammed against her ribs. "Yes."

"When you're ready...will you tell me?"

The air around her was thick, shimmering, liquid. She had to fight to speak through it.

"Yes," she whispered.

"Then I can wait." He smiled at her slowly, and her body felt weightless. She closed her hands around the sofa cushion beneath her, as if that could keep her from floating away.

"Here you are," her cousin Kate said, coming into the room. "The group sing's about to start downstairs and they're asking for you."

Allison had to repeat the words in her mind before they made any sense. "We'll be right down," she said in a voice she didn't recognize.

"I'll let them know," Kate said, glancing at Rick. "Unless you'd rather I said you were... busy?"

"No," she said quickly, jumping to her feet. "We're coming."

"Group sing?" Rick asked, following her out of the room.

"I apologize in advance," Allison said as they went down the stairs. She could feel her composure returning. "You're about to be subjected to a Landry family tradition. Whenever we get together for a party, someone starts singing Irish songs. We don't have to stay for it, though. If you want, we could say our goodbyes and—"

"Not a chance," Rick said firmly. "We're singing. I've been told I have a pleasant baritone voice, and we might as well put it to good use."

Half an hour later Rick had downed his third shot of Irish whiskey and was singing arm in arm with her dad and her uncle Sean. She took the opportunity to grab Jenna away from the musicians' circle and pull her into the kitchen.

"I need you to come shopping with me," she said without preamble.

Jenna stared at her. "Right now?"

"No, not now. Tomorrow. I need something to wear to a charity ball."

Jenna leaned against the counter. "Would Rick be taking you to this ball?"

"Yes."

She folded her arms. "Why don't you just wear something you already have? What makes this event so special?"

Allison glared at her. "Stop trying to make a point and say you'll go with me. I suck at shopping and I need your help."

"Fine, fine. What kind of dress are you looking for?"

"I want…" She hesitated. "I want a dress that will send a message." She took a deep breath. "I want something feminine. Something that says I'm in the mood to be romantic."

"As opposed to all those masculine dresses

that say I'm in the mood for a monster truck rally?"

"Will you be serious?"

Jenna grinned. "Sorry. I'm just trying to make up for the last ten years, when I haven't been able to tease you about guys. But of course I'll help you. We'll go to that new boutique downtown and find a dress that will make Rick's head explode."

"I don't need his head to explode. I just need him to know that I'm…"

Ready. She needed Rick to know she was ready.

Because she was. Sometime in the last half hour, watching his dark head tilt back as he drank a shot of whiskey, listening to him sing ballads with her family, catching his eye when he turned his head to look for her, she'd made her decision.

She knew it wouldn't last forever. Rick's relationships were never more than temporary, and she couldn't expect that to change. In fact, she fully expected to be left with a broken heart...the kind she might never recover from.

But for the first time in her life, she didn't care about the future. She didn't care about the consequences. She wanted Rick, and she was going to have him.

At least for a little while.

Chapter Ten

She made him helpless.

It was the one thing he'd worked his entire life to avoid, and there wasn't a damn thing he could do about it. His body was hard and hot when he was with her, his mind dense with images when they were apart. He worked in a fog, got through the day in a fog, except when the fever of desire burned through and he imagined making love to Allison until she was every bit as helpless as he was.

He'd never felt like this before. He wanted to

send her flowers, buy her jewelry, do all the things men had done for centuries when they wanted a woman so badly they couldn't think straight. The entire world seemed to glow, his desire for Allison coloring everything he saw and heard and touched, until the beat of blood through his veins seemed to echo in the air around him.

And he couldn't act on it. The next step of their relationship was in her hands, and he couldn't rush her. If he wanted to earn her trust he had to go at her pace.

They talked once or twice a day, and every night before they went to sleep. One of them would call to say hi, and before they knew it, an hour or more had gone by.

They saw each other twice that week, once for lunch and once with a group of her friends. On Thursday he had a late meeting and on Friday Allison answered phones for a telethon, so they didn't get to see each other. By

Saturday he was so impatient to be with her again that he pulled up at her apartment building twenty minutes early to pick her up for the charity ball.

He couldn't go up yet, so he settled back in the driver's seat with the radio on. He was thinking about Wednesday, when he'd gone to movie night at her apartment, and how cute she'd looked curled up in a corner of the couch with her feet tucked under her. He'd sat next to her for most of the evening, trying to watch the movie and not the way her face lit up when she laughed.

It had been hard being that close and not touching her, but how much harder would it be tonight?

Wednesday had been fun and casual. Tonight was black tie and champagne, men in tuxedos and women in gowns, a thirty-piece orchestra and a bachelor auction. The whole damn night was themed around couples and romance.

He remembered her threat to wear puce and orange. Considering her sense of humor, the odds were better than even that she'd do it. He started to grin, picturing Allison on a quest to find the ugliest dress in existence, just to tease him. He imagined festoons of taffeta, feathers, sequins...and Allison's face laughing up at him.

She'd still be the most beautiful woman he'd ever seen.

He checked his watch: six-thirty on the dot. Time to find out what she'd chosen for the occasion.

Allison had never spent an entire day just indulging herself. She'd answered phones for the telethon until midnight, so she slept late this morning, waking with a smile on her face, thinking about Rick. She stretched luxuriously, still smiling, before she got out of bed and made herself brunch.

Early in the afternoon she went to a salon for a manicure and pedicure. It felt wonderful to be pampered, like last week when Jenna had taken her here for a massage and a facial and to get her legs waxed, something Allison had never done in her life.

Jenna had informed her that the little red bumps and irritation from the waxing would be gone by today, and she was right. Home again now, relaxing in a bubble bath, Allison leaned back in the tub and stretched out a leg, running a hand from her ankle to her knee to her ankle. Her skin was as smooth as glass.

She'd never taken so much sensual pleasure in a bath, so much pleasure in her own physicality. She took her time toweling herself dry, and then smoothing rose-scented lotion into every inch of her skin.

She listened to an Ella Fitzgerald CD while

she got dressed. Jenna had made her buy real French silk stockings, thigh high wisps of gossamer so fragile she held her breath pulling them on and attaching them to the garter belt Jenna had also insisted she buy. After they were finally in place she went to look at herself in the full-length mirror on the back of the closet door.

In the black lace bra and panties, garter belt and stockings, Allison felt downright sexy for the first time in her life.

She went into the bathroom to put on her makeup—not much, just a little eyeliner and shadow and some rosy lip gloss. Then it was time to put on her dress.

She was glad, now, that Jenna had convinced her to buy this one. It was black lace and strapless and slit to the middle of her thigh, and in the boutique she hadn't even wanted to try it on. But Jenna and the salesclerk both had insisted, and once Allison had seen herself in it she could hardly believe it was her.

The bodice was like a corset, outlining her torso and making her breasts look—well, good. The floor-length skirt was elegant and simple, except for the slit, which would have revealed her garter belt if it had been cut a few inches higher.

She'd practiced walking in her high-heeled sandals all week, so she wouldn't embarrass herself by tripping over her own feet. She felt comfortable in them now, and she tried a few dance steps around her living room while she waited for Rick to pick her up. Rachel was a ballroom dance nut and had shown her some basic moves at work this week.

She looked at the clock—six-thirty. Rick would be here any second.

Her heart began to pound.

Rick could hear music coming from Allison's apartment as he walked down the hallway. It was Ella Fitzgerald singing with Louis

Armstrong, and he whistled the melody as he knocked on the door.

A few seconds went by. Then the door swung open, and the whistle died on his lips.

Allison was wearing a strapless gown. Her arms and shoulders were bare, her skin like porcelain against the black lace. The top was tight, outlining her breasts and pushing them up a little, and when he realized he'd been staring at her cleavage for a good ten seconds he jerked his gaze away.

There was a twist of silk at her waist, and the lace skirt fell in a graceful column to the floor. It was narrow enough to restrict her movements if it hadn't been for the slit up the side.

The slim leg showing through was encased in a sheer black stocking. Her shoes were black patent leather with three inch heels.

His gaze traveled up her body again to her face. Her short hair had been brushed back and there were jeweled clips gleaming in it, the same sapphire blue as her eyes.

She was wearing makeup, light and subtle—something around her eyes that made them look even bigger than usual, and something on her lips that made them shine. Her cheeks were pink but he thought that was probably natural. Considering he was staring at her like a hungry wolf, he was surprised her face wasn't bright red.

He'd better pull himself together before he backed her up against the wall and took her gown off with his teeth.

"Nice dress," he said.

He was glad to see that Allison was smiling at him as opposed to, say, calling 911 or running for her life.

"Did you bring the smelling salts?"

"No," he said. "But I didn't realize how much I'd need them."

It was only a ten-minute drive to the hotel,

but the fact that they made it there alive was a minor miracle. Rick's eyes kept drifting to the passenger seat. Allison was sitting straight with her hands folded in her lap, and the contrast between her prim posture and the slit in her dress made his whole body tighten.

When he downshifted his hand was inches away from her thigh. It was so easy to imagine reaching out for her that he hung onto the gearshift until his knuckles turned white.

They pulled up in front of the hotel, and Rick was glad to have a minute in the cool night air as they crossed the sidewalk to the entrance. Once inside, he slid the velvet wrap off her shoulders to hand to the employee behind the coat check counter.

"You're wearing perfume," he said as they walked into the ballroom. He hadn't noticed in the car, but when he was taking off her wrap he'd leaned in close and caught the scent.

"It's not perfume exactly, it's rose-scented

lotion," she said as they reached their table and he pulled out her chair. "Do you like it?"

He liked it so much he wanted to lick it off her, but he didn't think that was the answer she was looking for.

"Yes," he said instead, snagging two glasses of champagne from a passing waiter.

He sat down next to her as the orchestra finished tuning up and began to play. They started with a Cole Porter song, and the parquet floor filled up quickly.

Some of the city's most beautiful women were out there, but he only had eyes for Allison. "Do you want to dance?"

She got that deer in the headlights look he knew so well, and he thought she might say no. Then she took a quick gulp of champagne and set her glass back on the table.

"Yes," she said with determination. "I'd love to."

Almost immediately, her look of resolve

melted into her previous look of anxiety. "Or not. I mean…I'm not a very good dancer."

"That's all right," he said, rising to his feet and holding out his hand. "I am."

"You are?"

"It's one of my many talents."

He led her to the edge of the dance floor and turned her to face him. He guided her left hand to his shoulder and put his right hand on her waist. He started them off with a simple sway back and forth, to get the rhythm.

Her body was tense and she was frowning at his chest, her teeth sunk in her lower lip.

"You don't need to concentrate so hard."

"Sorry," she said, looking up at him. "I'm not good at being bad at things, if that makes any sense, so I'm overcompensating. I'll try to relax."

"Don't try," he said. "Don't think about it. Just listen to the music and look at me."

So she did. And now her blue eyes were

wreaking as much havoc on him as her body was in that dress.

But it was working. He could feel her relaxing, and moving with the music.

"Okay, that's good," he said. His voice was a little husky and he cleared his throat. "I'm going to try some steps now, all right? If I take a step forward like this, you just take a step back. That's it. And if I step to the side…see how easy it is? Now we're dancing."

He was only doing a simple fox-trot, but even so, it felt like no time before they were moving together like they'd been doing this forever.

That's what being with Allison was like. Like they'd known each other forever, and like everything he did with her was new.

She was relaxing more and more, following his lead as if she trusted him. He smiled down into her eyes and she smiled back at him, radiant and glowing. His hand around her waist tightened a little.

Her eyes were shining, her lips parted. "This is so fun," she said breathlessly. "I've always wanted to dance like this, to a real orchestra. It's like being in a Fred Astaire movie. Can we keep going? I mean, do we have to stop after this song?"

"We can keep going," he said, guiding her into their first turn. She followed his lead perfectly.

"That's good," he said. "The more you trust me, the more you'll be able to relax and let the music move through you."

"I trust you," she said softly, and her blue eyes were serious this time.

"You do?"

"I do."

"All right, then," he said, his hand tightening on hers. The orchestra had moved into "Fever", and the vocalist singing sounded exactly like Peggy Lee. The mood as well as the lyrics were a little too close for comfort right now, so he'd better kick the dancing into high gear to keep from kissing Allison right here on the dance floor.

"I'm going to get a little fancy now," he warned her. "Are you ready?"

Her eyes sparked and her chin went up. "I'm ready," she said, her voice strong and shaky at the same time, and the significance of those particular words didn't hit him until he was halfway through a series of spinning steps that took them toward the center of the dance floor.

I'm ready.

He froze in the middle of a glide, and Allison bumped into another couple.

I'm ready, she'd said. Not just the words, but the look in her eyes…

The man and his partner had turned.

Dancing be damned—he was going to get Allison alone right now to ask her what she'd meant by those words. Just as soon as he apologized to that couple for…

It occurred to him that only he and the other woman were saying the polite nothings this kind of situation called for. Allison and the man she'd bumped into were staring at each other as if they'd each seen a ghost.

After a second's mental effort Rick recognized him as Paul Winthrop, an attorney who worked in the patent law office his company utilized.

"Paul, it's good to see you again."

No response at all. Paul and Allison might have been the only two people in the room.

"Honey?" the woman asked after another moment of awkward silence. "Do you want to introduce me to your…friend?"

"Uh…" He tore his eyes away from Allison and turned to his companion. "Of course," he said, looking and sounding flustered. "Marian, this is…Allison. Allison Landry. She and I went to high school together. Allison, this is Marian Sanchez, my fiancée."

Allison's face was white and frozen, but she managed a nod in answer to Marian's polite hello.

The wheels were starting to turn in Rick's mind. Paul Winthrop…high school. Jenna had said her boyfriend's name was Paul. And while the thick head of blond hair was gone, replaced by a short cut and a receding hairline, he could see the resemblance to the prom picture in Allison's photo album.

Allison turned to him. "I'm going to visit the powder room," she said. Her voice was trembling. "I'll see you back at the table."

And without another word she was gone, moving quickly, almost stumbling, as she made her way through the dancing couples and back toward the lobby.

Rick stared after her for a minute before turning back to Paul. The wave of jealousy he felt was almost crippling, it was so swift and hot and blinding. How the hell could this balding lawyer have such a hold on her after so many years?

His hands clenched into fists. "How often have you two seen each other since high school?"

"Never," Paul said in a low voice. "This is the first time I've seen Allison in ten years."

He looked upset…almost sick to his stomach. Rick would have felt better if he seemed unaffected by the meeting. Judging by the expression on his fiancée's face, so would she.

The hot, nauseating rush of anger was making him shake. It felt familiar, too, in a horrible way, like remembering a nightmare. He'd better get the hell out of here before he said or did something unforgivable.

"Excuse me," he said abruptly. He left the dance floor and went to the restroom. It wasn't until he was staring at his reflection in the bathroom mirror that he realized what was so familiar about this feeling.

He looked like his father.

Gripping the edge of the sink with his hands, he remembered the senseless, jealous rages, when his father had accused his mother of being with other men.

Shaking his head, he forced himself to calm down. A momentary flash of jealousy didn't mean he was turning into his father.

He just needed to forget about Paul and think about Allison.

His mind went back to the moment before they'd bumped into the other couple, the moment on the dance floor when Allison had looked up at him with such resolve in her eyes.

I'm ready.

If that meant what he thought it did, an army of balding lawyers wouldn't stop him from being with her.

He made his way back to their table, but Allison wasn't there. Carol and her husband had arrived, and Derek was there with his date, and Rick made small talk for as long as he could stand it. Then he excused himself and went to look for Allison.

Allison paced back and forth across the empty conference room she'd found near the lobby. Her arms were wrapped around her waist and her stomach was in knots.

Why should she let Paul affect her like this? He'd hurt her once, why should he get to do it again?

Because she'd never dealt with it. She'd done exactly what Rick had done with his pain— denied it, ignored it, refused to give it any place in her conscious mind.

She remembered that night in the hospital, after she'd sent her parents away to be with Megan. She'd lain awake with tears leaking out of her eyes, her injuries making it so painful to move she hadn't been able to wipe them away.

There were tears in her eyes now, she realized, just as Rick came through the doorway.

They stared at each other for a moment. Her heart was beating so painfully her chest ached.

"I'm sorry, I don't feel well," she said as she brushed past him. "I'm going to take a cab home."

"Allison, wait. At least let me—"

She almost ran across the lobby toward the front doors.

Rick was behind her, calling her name. She couldn't face him now, she just couldn't.

All she could think of was the night she'd broken up with Paul. He'd been drinking—one of the many reasons she'd ended their relationship. It was after the spring concert at Fisher Academy and the school was mostly deserted.

She'd tried to run, but he was faster and stronger than she was. She'd made it outside to the soccer field but he'd grabbed her by the equipment shed and dragged her inside.

The hotel door was held open by an employee, and she walked swiftly through. Relief swept through her once she was outside, but then she realized she didn't have her purse—or money for a taxi.

She'd have to go back inside, but not right now. She couldn't face Rick, and she didn't want to deal with people.

To her left a tree-lined walkway led around the side of the hotel. Other than tiny white fairy lights strung on the trees, the path was in shadow. She hurried down it, walking and then running, until she found herself in a walled garden.

Dead end. She didn't see a way out, other than the way she'd come. Before she could get her bearings, Rick was there. "Allison!"

She retreated into the far corner of the garden, even though she knew there was no escape that way. Her hands clenched into fists as her thoughts, despite her almost violent efforts to keep them in the present, wrenched back to that night ten years ago.

He followed her. "Allison, are you all right?"

"I'm fine." Her arms were wrapped around her middle, and her muscles felt tense to the point of rigidity.

"No, you're not." Rick put a hand on her shoulder and she twisted away from him, backing up when there was nowhere to go. There was a brick wall behind her, and Rick in front of her.

And no place else to run.

Rick went still. It was dark where they were, but he could still make out the fear and panic on Allison's face. He took a step back.

"I'm fine. You didn't have to follow me. I was just looking for a way out." She took a deep breath. "I want to go home."

"Because of Paul?"

There was a long silence.

"Allison, I'm not going to stop you from leaving if that's what you want. I just wish you'd talk to me first, tell me what's going on. Then I'll drive you home myself if you want. Okay?"

They stood there in silence for a moment. He wanted to touch her, to comfort her, but he forced himself to keep his hands at his sides. He knew he couldn't crowd her right now.

"Okay," Allison said finally.

He felt a quick rush of relief. He looked around, and saw a wrought iron bench several yards away. He went over to it, and Allison followed. He was careful to leave a foot of space between them when they sat.

"So can you tell me why seeing Paul upset you so much?"

The trees in the garden had been strung with tiny white lights, winking like stars among the leaves. They created a dim, ambient radiance, enough that he could see Allison's expression.

Her face was tense and unhappy. When she spoke, her voice sounded hopeless.

"It's not important," she said softly.

His jaw tightened. "It is important. *You're* important. And why shouldn't you be upset? You saw an old boyfriend you haven't seen in ten years. A guy you're still in love with." He knew he sounded bitter, but he wasn't sorry he'd spoken the words out loud. Why not get it out in the open?

She shifted on the bench to face him. "Is that what you think? That I'm in love with Paul?"

His heart twisted. "It's true, isn't it?"

"No," she said, her voice trembling. "God, no."

She took a deep breath and let it out. "I *was* in love with him, once. Back in high school, when we found out Megan was sick." She shook her head slowly. "The next two years were so hard. She got worse and worse…and we found out we were going to lose her…and

I felt so dead inside, so lost, and I was trying to stay strong for her and for my parents…and sometimes I just wanted to run away. To forget about all the sadness and feel like a normal teenager for a while.

"You asked me at my parents' house, remember? You asked me if I had something in my life that wasn't about Megan or my family. Well, I did. I had a crush on Paul, and when he asked me out, I was so happy. I really was infatuated with him, in the beginning.

"But it wasn't real. I was using the relationship as an escape from everything else that was going on, and Paul… He hated that I spent so much time with Megan and my family. He said that he should be the most important thing in my life. He was used to getting everything he wanted," she said bitterly. "His father was Senator Winthrop, and Paul always had everything handed to him on a silver platter. I guess he thought I should be, too.

"For a while I gave in to him, and spent less time with my family. Every hour I spent with him was an hour I could have spent with Megan. For years I hated myself for that, for how much time and emotion I'd wasted on someone who wasn't worth a damn.

"We'd been going out for almost a year when he started pressuring me to have sex. I thought maybe if we slept together it would make things better between us. I thought if I gave him this thing he wanted so much, maybe he wouldn't resent the time I spent with Megan. But it made things worse.

"The first time just hurt. The second time I was tense, and Paul had been drinking and he wasn't exactly patient, so that hurt, too. It never got any better. I used to get sick to my stomach when he'd pick me up for dates."

He reached for her hand, closing his fingers around hers, and she didn't pull away. "After a few months of that I…I finally broke up with him." She paused. "I swore afterward I'd never put myself through anything like that again. I hated myself for having gone out with him at all, for having been so stupid. I swore I'd never waste another second of my life like that, when I could spend time with family, or friends, or doing work I loved."

She paused again. "When I saw him tonight, it reminded me of how stupid I was."

Rick shook his head. "How old were you then, seventeen? You weren't stupid, you were just a kid. You were a kid doing the best you could, and you did a better job with the load you had to carry than anyone had a right to expect—including you."

He tightened his hand around hers. "Do you remember when we were at the hospital, and you told me I shouldn't judge myself for the way I reacted to grief? You're always giving people permission to be human, Allison—everyone but yourself."

There was a long silence. They sat quietly, holding hands, until he heard her take a deep, shuddering breath.

"I've never talked about Paul," she said. "Not to anyone."

"You don't like talking about yourself. Not personal things."

"I know. I don't mean to be closed off or anything, it's just…I think you're probably right. I don't always let myself be human. In my work I'm always telling people to open up, to be vulnerable, when I can't do it myself."

He stroked her wrist with the pad of his thumb. "I'm glad you talked to me tonight."

"So am I." She hesitated. "But I'm sorry about your charity ball. Aren't you supposed to be in there hosting or emceeing, or something? As opposed to sitting out here in the dark with me?"

He smiled. "I turned the hosting duties for

318 THE MILLIONAIRE'S WISH

this event over to my VPs years ago. They enjoy it more than I do."

"Still…I know I ruined your night."

"I wouldn't say that."

He turned her hand palm up. Then he ran his fingertips softly over her skin, from her wrist to the inside of her elbow. He heard her breath catch. When he did it again, he felt her shiver.

When he thought about how Paul had pressured her and rushed her and hurt her, he had to clamp down on his anger. That's why she froze up sometimes, why she'd bolted the first few times he'd touched her.

He didn't want her body carrying any memories of Paul. He wanted to give her new memories, memories of the way it should be between a man and a woman.

Except he wasn't sure of that himself, anymore. All the women he'd been with, all the physical pleasure he'd given and received—nothing had prepared him for the way he felt when he was with Allison. This was uncharted territory for both of them.

Her skin was impossibly soft. He brushed his fingertips higher, up her arm to her shoulder. She didn't pull away, so he traced a path across her collarbone, every nerve in his body attuned to her. He felt every tremble, heard every hitch in her breathing.

Allison couldn't think about anything but this. Every cell of her body was focused on Rick, on his fingertips stroking softly along her skin. When he brushed over the inside of her elbow she quivered. When he drew his fingers across her collarbone she felt it in her nipples, already so hard she could feel them pushing against her dress.

"There's one thing I wanted to ask you," he said.

She swallowed. "What is it?" she asked, her voice husky.

He still held her right hand in his. "You said something on the dance floor before we bumped into Paul. Something about being ready. Do you remember?"

Of course she did. It was the thing she'd been trying to say from the moment he'd picked her up at her apartment.

"I remember," she said.

"What did you mean by that?"

Her confidence had been building all evening, until seeing Paul had shattered it completely. But now...

It wasn't that her confidence had returned. It was more that she wanted Rick so much it didn't matter anymore.

He was here, with her, in her personal heart of darkness. He'd listened to her and comforted her, but he'd done more than that. He'd taken darkness itself and transformed it, made it a place of sweetness and desire instead of pain.

She hadn't told him everything. A part of her still clung to that last secret, that last hidden place in her heart. She wanted to tell him, but she knew she needed a little more time before she crossed that last difficult breach.

She knew it would be hard for Rick to hear. She knew it would remind him of the violence in his own childhood. But she knew that when she was ready, he would listen to her.

He was waiting for her to speak right now. But for this particular declaration, she wanted to use body language.

She pulled her hand from his so she could put both palms flat on his chest, inside his jacket and over his shirt. She felt him still at her touch, and then take a deep breath. But he didn't move, and she knew the next step was up to her.

She ran her hands slowly up his chest, feeling the hard muscles beneath the smooth shirt. She let her hands move to his face, cupping his cheeks and brushing a thumb across his lips. She felt him shudder, and she smiled as she threaded her fingers through his hair. She'd been wanting to do that for days, and she was amazed to find it was as soft as it looked.

She leaned forward to place a soft kiss on his jaw. She felt his hands settle on her hips, as if he couldn't help himself anymore.

He smelled so good. He always smelled good, but right now the scent of aftershave on his skin turned her muscles to water. She pulled his head down and kissed him on the mouth.

He groaned, and his hands tightened on her hips. She moved closer, her breasts brushing against his chest, and he pulled her flush against him. He opened his mouth, and because their lips were pressed together hers opened, too.

The taste of him was wild and sweet and familiar. His hands roamed as if they couldn't rest in one place, over her waist, her back, her arms, her shoulders. Then he slid his fingers into her hair.

The kiss was hungry now, feverish. She was gripping the rigid muscles of his shoulders, and she was amazed at the strength under her fingers and the restraint that made his touch so gentle.

When he broke the kiss, they were both gasping. Rick rested his forehead against hers as they fought for breath.

After a minute he straightened up. "Allison."

Her breathing was still ragged, but she could speak. "Yes."

"Do you want to go back to the party?"

"No."

"Do you want to call it a night?"

She gripped the lapels of his tuxedo. "No."

He stroked her hair, letting his hand settle at the back of her neck. "Then I need you to tell me what you do want."

"I want—" She reached for her courage, and found she had more than enough. "I want you. I want to be with you."

His chest rose as he took a deep breath. "They have rooms here," he said.

"I hope so. I mean, it is a hotel."

"Do you—"

"Yes."

He grabbed her hand and pulled her to her feet.

When they were back inside the lobby she went to the coat check counter to retrieve her purse. By the time she got it, Rick was waiting for her.

He held up a hotel key card with a grin. Then he took her by the hand and led her to the elevators.

"Rick, I need to tell you…"

He looked down at her, and the heat in his gaze made her stomach flutter.

"You can tell me anything."

"It's just… I'm not sure I can… It's been a long time for me. I want to spend the night with you, but I'm not sure I'm ready for…"

"Hold that thought for a second," he said as the elevator doors opened and he pulled her inside.

When the doors closed again he backed her against the wall and kissed her, his hands thrust into her hair and his tongue stroking the inside of her mouth.

Her bones melted as she kissed him back, sliding her arms around his waist and pulling him closer.

He broke the kiss before she was ready and she made a little sound of protest.

"This is what I want to do tonight," he whispered. "I want to be alone with you, and kiss you, and do everything you're ready for and nothing you're not. Okay?"

She didn't trust herself to speak, so she just nodded. Rick smiled and leaned close again, but then the elevator came to a stop and the doors opened, so he took her hand instead and led her across the hall to another set of elevators.

Rick inserted his key card into a slot and the doors opened, this time for a short ride up just one floor.

When the doors opened again, Allison found herself looking into an opulent two-room suite with a wall of windows overlooking the city. She gasped, and Rick smiled with obvious pleasure at her reaction. "I thought you'd like it."

He went over to the mahogany entertainment console, turning on the satellite radio and finding the station he wanted. Frank Sinatra was singing "They Can't Take That Away From Me," and he turned back to Allison, walking toward her with his hand outstretched.

She took it, and he pulled her into his arms. They danced around the big living room with the city lights glinting through the picture windows, and her blood seemed to be shimmering instead of flowing through her veins.

There was a knock on the door, and Rick led her over to the couch before he went to go answer it.

"Pajamas," he said as he came back, carrying two white boxes, one large and one small.

"Wow," she said, smiling up at him. "I didn't realize you could order pajamas like room service."

"I asked downstairs if they'd raid the hotel boutique for us."

Her heart warmed. "Thanks," she said.

He sat down beside her, taking off his jacket and loosening his tie, and Allison realized why the look was so familiar.

"You look exactly like you did in that picture. The one in *People*."

He groaned. "Don't remind me."

"You looked so sexy," she said, leaning back

against the cushions and smiling at him. "The week after we had dinner that first night, I stole Rachel's copy of the magazine and brought it home with me."

He raised an eyebrow. "You did?"

"I did."

He grinned at her. "I still have that issue of the *Gazette*, the one with the pictures of us. And I keep your book on my night table. I stare at your face every night before I go to sleep."

"You do?"

"I do."

There was a moment of silence between them, charged and electric, and Allison reached for the box that held her pajamas to break the tension.

"I think I'll go put these on," she said.

"I was hoping you might indulge me in one thing first."

She swallowed. "What would that be?"

"Ever since you opened your apartment door tonight, I've been wanting to unzip that dress."

Her heart thumped against her ribs. "Just unzip it?"

He nodded.

After a moment's hesitation she moved over next to him and turned her back. She felt his hands against her bare skin, and then the slow slide of the zipper. He pressed a kiss against the nape of her neck and she got goose bumps on top of goose bumps.

"Let me take off your shoes," he said in a voice that made her knees weak, and she put a hand to the top of her dress to make sure it stayed up as she scooted back to her side of the couch, reclining back against the armrest and lifting her feet into his lap.

He slid the sandals off slowly, one after the other.

Her small feet seemed lost in his big hands as he stroked his thumbs across her insteps, over and over, a sensation so exquisite she had to close her eyes, unable to do anything but feel. When his hands moved higher, over her ankles and along her calves, she started to quiver.

She wanted him to go higher. She wanted to invite him into all her secret places. There was a sudden throbbing of heat and wetness at her center, a wild longing to open for him, to let him into the very heart of her.

"You should go get changed," he said after a moment.

She got to her feet a little shakily. "Can I show you something first?"

He raised an eyebrow. "That's a question you never have to ask."

The pile of the carpet felt thick and luxurious under her stocking feet. "My sister made me buy this black lace garter belt…"

She paused, keeping one hand on the bodice of her dress as she slowly pulled up her skirt.

"When I was putting it on, I had this fantasy of you seeing it."

The top of the slit rose to her hip, showing the black strap against her bare skin and the ribboned clasp holding up the top of her stocking.

The look in his eyes was more than she'd imagined in her fantasy.

"What doesn't kill us makes us stronger," he murmured. "I'd like to think that by continuing to sit here and not undoing that thing with my teeth, I'm building character."

"Character is important," she said, her voice husky. She took a deep breath. Then she put both her hands at her sides and let her dress slip to the floor.

For a second he just stared at her. Then he rose to his feet, moving slowly and deliberately, and closed the space between them.

When she felt his hands on the bare skin of her waist, she gasped.

"I don't know how I got through last week," he whispered. His eyes were on hers, the pupils so dilated they looked black. "I want you so much. I've wanted you from the moment I saw you."

His hands moved slowly up her sides, and she felt a restless ache start between her legs. "Me, too," she said indistinctly, her voice shaking.

"Liar," he said, leaning closer. "You thought I was a jerk the first time we met."

"And the second time, if we're being honest…"

He smiled, his hands stopping just under her bra.

"And now?"

"Now I think you're…okay."

"Just okay?" His thumbs moved, caressing the undersides of her breasts through the lace of her bra. Desire stabbed through her, leaving her knees weak.

"Definitely better than okay."

"How much better?"

His hands moved higher, and she held her breath. When his thumbs stroked across her aching nipples, a spasm rocked her body.

Her knees buckled, but before she could collapse he scooped her into his arms as if she weighed nothing at all.

She rested her head against his chest as he carried her into the bedroom. Her hand found a gap between the buttons of his shirt and she slid inside, touching his bare skin, where she could feel his heart pounding against her fingers.

He laid her down on the bed and covered her body with his own, kissing her fiercely, hungrily, his tongue tangling with hers and his weight pinning her to the mattress.

She wanted him closer. She opened her legs and wrapped them around his waist. She felt the length of his erection pressed against her center and she knew that was what she wanted, needed, craved on such a primal level she hardly recognized the wild sound that escaped her throat.

He buried his face in the crook of her neck for a second, saying her name against her skin. Then his hands were underneath her, at the clasp of her bra, and in the second after it was gone his mouth was on her breast.

She cried out, arching her back, and then he was circling one nipple with his tongue while he caressed the other with his fingers, stroking until she was pushing herself against him, unable to stay still.

He kissed between her breasts and lower, and when he got to her garter belt she heard it rip. "I'll buy you another one," he said, and then he was tugging her panties and her stockings down her legs.

Before she knew what was happening he'd hooked her knees over his shoulders and his mouth was on her again, so intimately this time she twisted away in instinctive shyness.

But his strong hands were on her hips as he held her in place against him, against his mouth, his tongue, and her motions intensified the sensation until she was moving with him, rocking with him, doing everything his hands urged her to do as a new kind of pressure started to build inside her.

Her hands fisted in the sheets as she fought to breathe, and the pressure tightened and coiled in every muscle. When the explosion came she called out his name, her head thrown back, the wave of pleasure so intense it left her shaking.

She came down slowly, sweetly, through layers of warmth and pleasure. She'd come undone and Rick was weaving her together again, moving up her body with exquisite slowness, kissing her as softly as snow falling on snow.

When he made it all the way up she'd regained some muscle control, and she wrapped her arms around his neck as he kissed her long and deep.

After a while he rolled onto his side, propping himself up on one elbow.

"I got a little carried away there," he said, reaching out a hand to brush the sweat-dampened hair from her forehead. "I meant to go slow, but you were so incredible...so responsive..."

She gave a long, shuddering sigh. "I didn't know I could be like that. I didn't know anything could feel like that." She took another breath, and then turned on her side to face him, her face pillowed on her arm. "We're not done, are we?"

He was still running his fingers through her hair. "We can be, if you're tired."

"I'm not tired at all. And you still have all your clothes on."

He smiled at her. "We've got all night, Allison. I can wait."

"I don't want to wait," she said. "I want you naked now. I dream about seeing you naked. I've been ogling you for weeks."

She sat up and put a hand on his shoulder, pushing gently until he lay flat on his back.

His eyes traveled down her naked body and back up to her face. "Now that you have me at your mercy, what are you going to do with me?"

"I'm going to take your clothes off," she said, reaching out to undo the top button of his shirt.

She took her time, her movements slow and precise, and when he actually growled at her she just smiled and moved onto the second, and the third. She undid them all, and then brushed her palms across the hard planes of his chest as she slid the shirt off his shoulders. He shifted so she could pull it off completely, and then lay back down as she leaned forward to kiss her way up his torso. She could feel his heart pounding.

"Allison, you're killing me," he said, reaching for her.

"I'm not done yet," she told him, catching his arms and putting them back down by his sides. Then she lowered his zipper and tugged his pants down his legs, letting him kick them off once they were past his knees.

"Black silk boxers," she said, a little breathlessly. "Very sexy." She took hold of the waistband and slid them down and off, helping him shed his socks, too.

Only then did she let herself look at him, really look at him, at his long, hard-muscled body and the erection jutting out from his hips.

For the first time, she felt a little nervous.

He rose up on his elbows, and the hunger in his eyes made her tremble.

She scooted up the bed so she could stretch

out next to him. "Maybe you can take over for a while," she said.

He gave her a quick, hard kiss. "I can do that. But I want you so much right now I'm shaking. I'm afraid I'll lose control."

She met his gaze steadily. "I want you to lose control."

He swallowed. "One second," he said, reaching down to the floor for his pants and the condom in his wallet. He tore open the foil package and covered himself, and then he was back at her side.

The few moments they hadn't been touching seemed like too long.

She gripped him by the shoulders and tugged him down. For a moment she felt his body hard on hers, her breasts crushed against his chest. Then he pulled back, supporting his weight on his arms.

"Are you sure you're—"

She opened her legs for him and felt his hips

slide into the cradle of hers, his hard length pressing against her center.

He closed his eyes briefly. "I guess you are."

A moment later he was at her entrance, his arms corded and tight as he held himself rigid above her. Then slowly, carefully, he pushed inside.

Her eyes closed as her body stretched to accept him, inch by inch. They both went still as he pushed deeper, her body hot and tight around his. Then he was home, all the way home, and her eyes flew open to meet his.

"Rick," she said, her voice ragged and trembling and full of wonder.

His eyes never left hers as he began to move, sliding out and pushing in, and she felt the shock every time he found her center. When the pressure started to build she moved beneath him, restless and agitated, and Rick's jaw tightened as his thrusts turned harder, faster. When the storm broke this time she knew he'd be right there with her.

Her head arched back as she cried out. Her body spasmed and then fluttered around him. He called out her name and thrust hard once more, bringing his mouth down on hers as he pulsed inside her.

It was a long time before they moved again.

Her body was still humming when he eased out of her, taking care of the condom before he lay down beside her again. He pulled her close, and she rested her head on his chest with a feeling of joy inside her that was too big for words. His arms tightened around her, and she wondered if he was feeling the same thing.

She fell asleep listening to the sound of his heartbeat.

When she woke up, it was a few hours before dawn.

She lay in Rick's arms for a few blissful

minutes, and then sat up carefully so she could watch him sleep. His strong features looked relaxed, peaceful even, with those intense green eyes hidden from view. In the low light of the desk lamp they'd left on, his hair was coal black.

Allison hugged her knees to her chest and settled in for a nice long look.

His mouth… He could work magic with that mouth. Hard one minute, soft the next, demanding and tender at the same time.

And his body… Allison let her gaze drift down over his arms and shoulders and chest to his well-toned abs and the hipbones angling down toward his…

He might be asleep, but she still blushed.

And his hands…oh, yes, his hands. Strong, knowing, gentle… He could chase away fears with a single caress, take her to heaven with one firm stroke.

Allison rested her chin on her knees. She

felt more at home with Rick, more at ease, than she'd ever felt with anyone. She'd told him things she'd never told a living soul—and she knew, now, she was going to tell him the rest. She'd tell him what happened the night she broke up with Paul.

A wall inside her crashed down and everything flowed together, whole.

Ever since that night ten years ago she'd kept her strength and weakness apart, the one hiding the other. A part of her strength had always come from the fear of weakness, the fear of needing something outside herself. But the strength coursing through her now was different. It came from everything that she was. Rick accepted every part of her, and because of that, she could too. She didn't have to be afraid of herself anymore.

A sudden rush of joy made her feel like dancing. She couldn't contain it. She had to tell Rick, had to tell him she—

"Rick!"

He awoke with a gasp, reaching out for her blindly. She grabbed both his hands in hers.

"Allison, what is it? What's wrong?" He pulled one hand away to scrub the sleep from his eyes, and she felt a wave of nervousness. Her epiphany had seemed so momentous, but maybe it could have waited until morning.

Except that it couldn't. *She* couldn't.

She straddled him. His body came alive, and suddenly his eyes didn't look sleepy at all.

"Feel free to wake me up like this anytime." He thrust up against her, and Allison had to stifle a moan even as she grabbed his hands and pinned them to his sides.

"Cut that out," she said sternly. "I have something to say to you."

He stared up at her, surprised. Waiting.

Such a simple thing. Three little words. Three…little…

She wanted to shout it. She wanted to sing it,

with a full orchestra behind her and fireworks in the sky. But with her breath all gone and her heart hammering against her ribs, her voice was hardly more than a whisper.

"Rick—"

She leaned closer, afraid he wouldn't hear her.

"Rick, I love you."

He went utterly, completely still. The planet might have stopped on its axis.

His eyes were bright, and she realized with a shock that there were tears in his eyes.

"I love you, too," he whispered. Then he gripped her wrists. "I love you, Allison," he said, his voice clear and strong this time.

Then he was tugging her down to him and his arms were tight around her, and they were kissing.

They kissed forever, like teenagers. They kissed like they were never going to stop.

They fell asleep in each other's arms, their

legs tangled together and Allison's head on Rick's shoulder.

When she woke up again, it was a new day.

Chapter Eleven

Rick opened his eyes and saw Allison coming toward him with a breakfast tray.

He sat up and propped his pillow behind him. "The woman I love brings me breakfast in bed after a night of incredible sex. Either I'm still asleep, or this is an elaborate plot to make me believe that dreams really do come true."

"It's the second thing," she said with a smile, putting the tray down next to him and sitting cross-legged on the bed. She'd put on her pajama top but not the bottoms, and the glimpse he caught of her black lace panties made him instantly aroused.

"You know—"

"Don't even finish that thought," she said, pouring him a cup of black coffee.

"How do you know what I was thinking?"

"Call it woman's intuition. Try to control yourself long enough to have breakfast, okay? And then there's something I want to tell you."

He grinned at her. "You already told me you love me. You're not going to take it back, are you?"

"Never," she said.

She handed him his coffee and poured a cup for herself, but she set it down on the tray without drinking it. "It's something about Paul," she said abruptly. "I told you a lot last night, but—" She trailed off.

"You don't have to talk about anything you're not ready to."

"I know," she said. "I appreciate that. But I'm ready to tell you now, because…" She broke off and smiled at him suddenly. "I realized this morning that it doesn't matter anymore. I've been carrying this around for so many years, like a wound that won't heal. And then I woke up beside you and realized that the memory doesn't have any power over me anymore. Because of you."

She pushed the tray aside and crossed the space between them, and he had just enough presence of mind to put his coffee on the nightstand before she was kissing him. He wrapped his arms around her and slid down so she fell across his chest, and he let his hands rove under her top and across the smooth skin of her back, and then down to her hips so he could fit her securely against the erection that the blankets weren't doing much to hide.

Another second of that and their conversation would have had to wait, but Allison broke the kiss and scooted a few feet away.

"Sorry," she said sheepishly.

"Yeah, that was terrible of you. Come here and do it again."

She smiled and shook her head. "Just let me get this all out, okay? Then I'll kiss you senseless, I promise."

He sat up against the headboard again. "It's a deal," he said.

"Thanks," she said. "So…" She took a deep breath. "It took me a long time, but I finally realized Paul wasn't making me happy. Whatever feelings I'd had for him in the beginning were gone. To make things worse, he—he drank a lot, and when he drank he got angry. He was drinking the night I broke up with him."

She was hugging her knees, her eyes looking down as she told the story. "He'd yelled at me a few times, but he'd never hit me. Not until that night."

Rick froze.

Allison's eyes were still down. "When I told him it was over, he slapped me across the face. I tried to run away, but I wasn't fast enough to get away from him. He dragged me into an equipment shed, and…"

She closed her eyes. "He hit me so many times. I think he kicked me, too, after I was on the ground. I had two broken ribs, a fractured collarbone, a broken wrist."

A white flash burst behind his eyelids, leaving him shaking.

"He left me there in the dark. I think I might have passed out for a little while. When I came to I dragged myself out, and found a pay phone, and called for a cab so I could get to the hospital."

"A cab?" he asked abruptly. "Why not your parents? Why not 911?"

She sighed. "I told my parents I took a bad fall off a horse. They were already losing a daughter to cancer… How could I give them one more horror to deal with? Especially since I felt like it was all my fault for going out with him in the first place, when I should have been focused on my family."

She held up a hand before he could say the obvious. "I know it wasn't my fault. I get that now, I really do. If I could go back in time and talk to myself I'd know exactly what to say. But I was eighteen, and I felt guilty and ashamed and sick of myself, and all I wanted to do was forget it ever happened. To put it behind me and never be vulnerable like that again."

He remembered telling her the reasons he never talked about his father, and felt sick inside. "But by not telling anyone, you were agreeing with him. You were agreeing that you were nothing, someone whose pain didn't matter."

"I know," she said softly. "Believe me, if something like that happened to me today, I wouldn't react the same way."

His throat felt raw, his muscles tense. If anyone dared to hurt Allison today he'd tear them to pieces with his bare hands.

"You never pressed charges?"

She shook her head. "A few days after it happened he got into a bar fight with some businessman. Hurt him pretty badly, I think. The case went to court and for the first time in his life Senator Winthrop couldn't make something go away. Paul spent some time in juvenile detention.

"I think it scared him straight," she added with a grim smile. "I'm pretty sure he must have gone through the twelve steps at some point, because I got a letter from him when I was in college, wanting to 'make amends' for what he'd done to me. I never answered it. Sometimes I wonder if I should have…not for his sake, but for mine."

He could never make amends for hurting Allison. For hurting a girl who'd never done harm to a living soul. A girl who tried so hard to take care of others, who'd grown into the most beautiful, compassionate, incredible woman he'd ever met.

He wanted to reach out for her, to pull her into his arms and take her away, take her… where? To a place where there was no violence, no evil, no demons masquerading as human beings?

There was no such place. He of all people should know that.

"I wish you'd told me this last night," he said.

She stared at him. "Why?"

"If you'd told me last night, I could have… talked to him."

Her eyes got wider. "What do you mean by

that? Rick, what are you thinking about right now?"

"Nothing."

"I don't believe you. You look…dangerous."

"I'm fine." He threw off the blankets and reached for his clothes, on the floor beside the bed. He got dressed quickly, as if there was somewhere he could go—something he could do.

There had to be something he could do.

Then he looked at Allison. She seemed so small and fragile sitting there on that enormous bed, her eyes wide as she stared at him.

"Should I—not have told you?"

He sat down again, taking her hands in his.

"I'm glad you told me. I love you, and you can tell me anything. It's just…thinking about that bastard hurting you, and you dealing with it all alone…"

His hands tightened.

"That's why you stayed single for ten years. Because of what he did to you."

"I never wanted to feel like that again. Not that I expected every guy to hit me, but…I saw my friends get hit by love in other ways, ways they brought on themselves. Wasting their time and their emotions like I had. Life hands you enough pain without standing in line begging for more."

She shook her head. "I didn't want to waste my heart on someone who wasn't worth it, someone who would hurt me. I didn't want to waste time on an illusion."

Paul had done that to her, made her feel that way. Made her turn her back on the very idea of love for ten years. He hadn't just hurt her physically; he hadn't just hurt her once. He'd hurt her over and over again.

The rage sweeping through him was so consuming that when she spoke again, it was hard to focus on her words.

"I was comfortable being single. I never felt like I was missing anything, not once. And then you came along…"

Those words, and the tone of her voice, cut through his emotions and made him see her again.

She was smiling. "You came along, and made me throw everything I'd ever believed out the window. Because of you, there's nothing lurking in the darkness anymore…only magic. The magic you make me feel."

He didn't know what to say. His heart ached in his chest, and he leaned forward to kiss her.

Allison had let her experience with Paul go. It was over for her. What she'd just shared with him had been the departing shadow of that bad memory, and he should let it go, too.

But instead of the peace he'd felt this morning, there was turmoil. And in his mind's eye all he could see was Paul Winthrop's face.

Then he remembered that the patent law office was in Chicago. Paul probably lived in Chicago. Chances were, he'd stayed over after the party. He could be in this hotel right now.

He stood up, his muscles trembling. "I'll be right back," he said. "I need to go…check on something."

"Rick—"

"I'll only be gone a minute," he told her. "I'll be back before you finish your breakfast."

When she looked in his eyes, Allison knew exactly what he was planning to do. She shot to her feet and blocked his way.

The expression on his face raised the hairs on the back of her neck.

"Let me go, Allison."

"Rick, you have to listen to me. You can't go after Paul. He's not worth it."

This was her fault. She should have realized that Paul might be staying over in the hotel, and that Rick might react this way. He'd watched his mother be abused, and she knew he had a protector personality.

Not being an alpha male herself, she hadn't thought about what a man like Rick might do when confronted with this information—especially when the person who'd hurt her could be right here in the hotel.

He tried to step around her, but she got in his way again.

His jaw was like granite. "Let me go."

"I can't. I'm afraid of what you'll do if you find him."

"Paul's the one who should be afraid. He deserves to feel every bit of fear you did that night."

"Maybe so. But he could file assault charges against you, Rick. You know I can't let you do this."

A muscle in his jaw jumped. "You can't stop me."

"How are you going to get past me? Push me aside? Walk right through me?"

"Damn it, Allison, get out of my way!"

"No."

"What makes you think I won't push you?" A spasm of pain crossed his face. "What makes you think I won't hurt you?"

"Because I know you."

"You don't. You don't know what's inside me."

His hands clenched into fists. There was so much rage and torment in his eyes that she couldn't stop herself from reaching toward him.

He took a quick step back. He was breathing hard, every muscle in his body tense.

"Stay away from me," he said.

"Rick—"

She could feel the tension in him, rising to the breaking point. He took another backward step and bumped against the dresser, jerking his head around and catching sight of his own face in the mirror.

He froze.

Allison could see his reflection over his shoulder. It looked like he was staring into an abyss, into the eyes of a demon that haunted his darkest nightmares.

He stood there for a minute. As she watched, she could see the rage leaving his body. When he turned around again, the look in his eyes brought her heart into her throat.

She'd seen that expression on the faces of people who'd just been given a terminal diagnosis.

She took a step toward him.

"Rick—"

"It's okay," he said, moving past her. "I'm not going after Paul."

Watching him leave was one of the hardest things she'd ever done. She wanted to follow him so much it hurt.

But not yet. She needed to give him a little time first, a little space.

And she thought she knew where he'd go to find it.

* * *

Rick drove straight to Hunter Hall. He didn't decide to consciously; he just got in his car and started the engine. It wasn't until he was halfway there that he realized where he was going.

There were two images in his mind. Allison waking him up in the middle of the night, leaning over him and saying those words with such determination, such knowledge of what they meant.

"I love you."

If he lived to be a hundred he'd never forget how it felt to hear her say that—and how it felt to say it back to her.

He tried to cling to that memory, to burn the other image out of his head.

The sight of his father's eyes looking out of his face.

He hated that Allison had seen him like that. But even though his rage hadn't been directed at her, it was something that was inside him. A part of him.

The poison his father had left behind. The violence he'd never be able to escape.

Allison deserved better than that. Better than a man with this ugliness inside him. He loved Allison with everything he was, every cell in his body—but hadn't his father loved his mother once? In the beginning?

With that legacy of hate in his heart, how could he ever trust himself completely?

Rick pulled up in front of Hunter Hall and turned off his engine. He sat in silence for a moment before he dropped his head into his hands.

"Richard? What are you doing here?"

He raised his head to see his grandmother standing in the driveway, peering at him through the window.

He got out of the car and slammed the door

364 THE MILLIONAIRE'S WISH

shut, leaning back against it and dragging a hand through his hair.

"Are you all right?"

"I'm fine." His voice was rough, and he cleared his throat. "Gran…there's something I have to tell you."

She tilted her head back to look at him. "Goodness, Richard. You look absolutely dreadful. What is it?"

"I lied to you. About Allison. We weren't really dating—not at first. I asked her to pretend we were, because I knew that was the only way I could get Hunter Hall."

She was quiet for a moment. "You felt you had to do that? Lie to me?"

He remembered talking to Gran on the phone, the day he'd first met Allison.

"I couldn't stand the idea of losing Hunter Hall. It's always felt like home, with you living here. But if you leave, and Jeremiah moves in…it won't be."

There was another silence.

"I'm partly to blame," she said slowly. "I hated seeing you alone, and I always wanted a family to live in this house. And I thought if I made my feelings clear, perhaps you'd at least consider dating a different type of girl—a girl you could actually fall in love with. I was hoping all along I wouldn't need to give the place to Jeremiah." She sighed. "I had no business trying to manipulate you like that. Considering the circumstances, I forgive you for lying to me."

She looked up at him, and while her green eyes might have been brighter fifty years ago, they couldn't have been any sharper. "What did you mean when you said you and Allison weren't really dating *at first?*"

He smiled a little. "Yes, Gran, my plan

backfired. My make-believe romance turned into reality. At least for a little while."

"I see. And now?"

He looked away. "It's not in the cards, Gran. You might as well call Jeremiah and tell him the good news."

She shook her head. "I've changed my mind about Jeremiah. I've never really liked him, or that dreadful wife of his—and there's no reason I would like their children any better, if they ever have any. I'd rather give this place to you, my dear—even if you live here alone all your days, and die a curmudgeonly old bachelor."

He stared at her. "But…why?"

"Well, you're my favorite grandson."

"I'm your only grandson."

"That, too," she said with a smile. "In any case, I'll be moving out within a month—and Hunter Hall will be yours. What are you going to do with it?"

He looked up at the gabled rooftops silhou-etted against the blue sky. With Hunter Hall in his possession, he now had everything he'd ever wanted.

He closed his eyes.

"I don't know," he said. "I don't know."

She reached up and put a hand on his cheek. "Why don't you take a walk, Richard? Take some time to clear your head. Down by the pond, perhaps. That was always a favorite spot of yours."

The pond was a quarter mile away. From here, he could just see the tops of the willow trees.

"Good idea," he said. He smiled down at his grandmother and gave her a quick kiss. "I love you, Gran. I don't think I tell you that enough."

"No, you don't. But I love you, too."

She watched him walk across the grounds

until he was out of sight. Then she went back inside the house to call Allison.

Allison went back to her apartment to shower and change. She took her time, counting every second. Only then did she let herself make the drive to Hunter Hall.

When she got there, Meredith answered the door.

For a moment the housekeeper just stared at her. Then she called out, "Evie! She's here… Allison's here!"

Meredith let her in, and there was a hurrying of footsteps before Rick's grandmother came into view.

"Thank goodness," she said. "I've left messages at the Star Foundation but of course no one's there today, and your home number is unlisted." She paused suddenly. "You did come to see Richard, didn't you? I've just been assuming, but…how did you know he was here?"

Allison took the elderly woman's hand. "Because this is where Rick goes when he's hurting."

Evie's eyes filled with tears.

"Can you tell me where he is?"

Evie nodded. "He's down by the pond," she said, leading Allison to a set of French doors opening onto the gardens. "If you follow that path, it'll take you there."

Rick was sitting on a stone bench, staring out at the water. He sat so still that Allison slowed to a halt, watching him.

A minute went by, and another. Allison knew she hadn't made a sound, but something made him look over his shoulder, and he saw her.

She moved toward him then, taking a seat on the bench. He was still in his black tuxedo pants and white dress shirt, wrinkled and stained now, and his jaw was rough with stubble.

"Allison," he whispered as if he couldn't believe she was there. Then he took her in his arms and kissed her hair, her cheeks, her eyelids, and finally her lips.

When he broke the kiss he pulled her even tighter against him, wrapping her up in a cocoon of warmth and strength. But she could feel his body shaking, and she knew he was feeling anything but strong right now.

"I'm sorry," he said, his words muffled against her hair. "I had to kiss you one last time."

She pulled away a little, enough so she could look at him. "Why does it have to be the last time?"

He didn't answer her right away. He took her hands in his and looked down at them, and when he spoke his voice was quiet.

"You know why. I know what you saw in my

face this morning, and I don't want you to see that again. I don't want you to look at me and see Paul."

"You're nothing like Paul."

"I don't want to look in the mirror and see my father."

"You're nothing like your father."

His eyes met hers. "Right after you bumped into Paul last night, I went into the bathroom and saw my reflection. That was when I thought you were still in love with him, and I was so jealous I…" He closed his eyes. "I looked exactly like him. And then, this morning…I could swear his eyes were looking out of my face."

He opened his eyes again. "You said there's nothing lurking in the darkness anymore. But for me, there's still something lying in wait. Something I'm not sure I'll ever be free of."

"Violence," she said.

"Yes."

"Rick, have you ever hurt someone weaker than you?"

"God, no," he said, a look of absolute revulsion in his eyes.

She smiled a little. "I wish you could have seen your face when I asked you that question. You're a strong man, and you'd fight for someone you love. But you're not capable of hurting an innocent."

"You can't know that for sure."

"Yes, I can."

"But how? How can you know that?"

She framed his face with her hands. "Because I know you. I trust you. I trust you with my life, Rick. With my hopes, my dreams, my heart."

He stared at her. "All of that?" he whispered.

"All of that."

His voice sounded shaken. "I don't trust myself, yet."

"I know. But I trust you enough for both of us."

He pulled her into his arms and hugged her close, so close she had to push against his chest after a moment.

"Oxygen," she gasped, laughing.

He laughed, too, a little shakily. "I love you, Allison. I love you so much. I wanted to give you everything, to lay the world at your feet, but you're the one with all the gifts—all the gifts that matter."

He took a deep breath. "There is one thing I'd like to give you, though. I'd like to change the name of this place."

"Change the name of Hunter Hall?"

"Yes. I'd like to call it Megan's House."

She stared at him.

He took her hands in his. "It's just an offer. Maybe you'll decide this isn't the right place for your center after all. Megan's House is your dream, and you're the only one who knows what will make it come to life."

Her head was spinning. "I can't… I don't…"

"You've spent your whole life making wishes come true for other people. It's time someone granted a wish for you."

Tears burned behind her eyelids. "But Hunter Hall is your family home. I know how much it means to you."

"It doesn't mean anything to me."

"But—"

"I always thought it did. This place was my holy grail…a piece of magic I could never really possess, a wish that would never really come true. Even when I thought it would be mine someday, something about it never seemed quite real.

"When I came here today, I realized why. It's because I thought, all these years, that what I wanted was the house. That the magic was in the house itself. But what I really wanted, what I really wished for, was what I always found here. Love, family, happiness, peace. But those things don't have anything to do with Hunter Hall—not the building, anyway. Those things are about people."

He cupped her face with one hand. "You're my grail, Allison. My every wish come true."

She covered his hand with hers and closed her eyes. She hadn't known it was possible for her heart to feel so full.

"Would you say it again?" he asked after a while.

She knew what he wanted to hear. "I love you."

"Again."

"I love you."

"Maybe you could just say it over and over until—"

She cut off his words with a kiss, and he wrapped his arms around her waist. "Or you could do that," he murmured against her mouth.

She kissed a path along his jaw. "Let's go tell your grandmother you're okay, and then let's find a room. I don't care where it is, as long as there's a bed in it."

He surged to his feet, pulling her up with him. "Your wish is my command."

Epilogue

Six Months Later

"What's going on with you, Richard?" his grandmother asked him. "You haven't stopped smiling all day."

"Why wouldn't I be smiling? Megan's House officially opened its doors today."

The two of them looked out over the grounds of the Hunter estate, where children and their families were enjoying the beautiful autumn afternoon. Allison was helping to flip burgers with Rachel and Jenna.

"Six months, and you still can't take your eyes off her," his grandmother said. "When are you going to take the final plunge and pro-pose?"

"Funny you should ask," Rick murmured. "See you later, Gran," he added as he moved purposely across the lawn.

He came up behind Allison and slid his arms around her waist.

"Take a walk with me," he said, as she twisted around to give him a quick kiss.

"Now? But the party—"

"Will be fine without us for a little while."

She cocked her head at him. "You're up to something," she said after a moment, smiling.

"That's a definite possibility," he admitted as he took her hand. He led her down to the pond and over to the stone bench where she'd found him that day six months ago.

They sat in silence for a minute, breathing in the dense sweet scent of fall and listening to the willow trees rustle in the breeze. Allison was watching a family of ducks glide by, a soft smile on her face.

He reached into his pocket and knelt down at her feet.

She stared at him, her eyes wide, and then down at the ring in the black velvet box lying open in the palm of his hand. It was a tiny flower made of jewels, one perfect diamond surrounded by sapphires.

"Oh, Rick," she breathed, looking back up at him.

His voice was strong, but there was a tremor in it, too. "Allison, will you marry me?"

She tried to speak and failed. Then she slid off the bench and into his arms.

"Yes," she said, her voice muffled against his shoulder. "Yes, yes, yes."

Rick closed his eyes and held her tight.

And when Allison pulled back so he could slip the ring on her finger, he knew that here, with her, he'd come to the very center of the labyrinth. He could see into the deepest reaches of his heart. And instead of the darkness he'd always feared, there was light, blinding light—and a love that would burn brighter every day.

* * * * *